Rourke wanted Aly
in the worst way

Every waking moment, he wanted to haul her to him, to make love to her. They were highly, explosively compatible. One kiss told them things they'd both have been better off never knowing. It had been a brash mistake. Rourke had known at once, and he'd been angry with himself the moment it was over.

The brief brush of their lips had told him how good they could be together—in bed and out. Something powerful and unforgettable had passed between them, and Aly had touched him in a way he'd never been touched by a woman. It excited him and nettled him and worried him.

Then Rourke reminded himself that he had nothing to give a woman . . . not in the shape he was in.

Renee Roszel freely admits that she stumbled onto the idea for *Devil To Pay* with the same dumb luck a turkey might stumble into a bird sanctuary the day before Thanksgiving. One evening at dinner, her friend and fellow writer Stephanie Woody suggested that she write about her family's auction firm. While researching, Renee found the exotic world of huge estates and million-dollar auctions fascinating—but not as fascinating as the hot-as-hell romance between her heroine and hero! Renee's most recent Temptation, *Unwilling Wife,* was nominated for Best Short Contemporary Romance of 1992 by the Romance Writers of America.

Books by Renee Roszel

HARLEQUIN TEMPTATION
246—ANOTHER HEAVEN
279—LEGENDARY LOVER
334—VALENTINE'S KNIGHT
378—UNWILLING WIFE

DEVIL TO PAY

RENEE ROSZEL

Harlequin Books

TORONTO • NEW YORK • LONDON
AMSTERDAM • PARIS • SYDNEY • HAMBURG
STOCKHOLM • ATHENS • TOKYO • MILAN
MADRID • WARSAW • BUDAPEST • AUCKLAND

To Fran Wilson
My husband's mother, and fellow writer,
who invited me to my first writer's club meeting.
Thanks, Fran—for shaping my life—
by giving me, first, a great husband,
and second, a great career!

Published December 1992

ISBN 0-373-25522-5

DEVIL TO PAY

1

ALYSSA HAD TWO RULES she lived by. Rule number one: Don't lose control. Rule number two: Don't screw up rule number one.

Today, she'd screwed up.

To her abject horror, the huge double doors to the Rountree mansion were standing open. Any lust-crazed, hacksaw murderer could sashay in and rape, pillage or hack as he pleased, and Aly was to blame.

Or, what was more likely, and what Aly really feared, was that due to her lapse, someone might have sneaked inside this vast treasure-filled mansion, and made off with hundreds of thousands of dollars' worth of property—property she and her staff had been hired to prepare and catalog for auction.

Angry with herself, Aly ground her teeth. As head of Bean Auction, she was in charge of security of this estate during her stay here. And on her first day, *her first minute,* she'd completely blown it! "Great security!" she muttered sarcastically. "Alyssa Bean Fields! How could you have been so stupid!"

Frustrated by the fact that there was nothing she could do about it now, she pushed sweat-dampened hair from her forehead and reentered the châteauesque mansion. It was cool inside. Of course, since it was 104 degrees outside, anything would be cool by comparison. But somehow this empty, echoing shrine to extravagance had the feel of a long-abandoned mausoleum.

The door creaked ominously as if chiding her for her unkind description, but she'd had a queasy feeling in the pit of her stomach ever since she'd come in. Like something life-threatening, or life-altering, was going to happen. Maybe that's why she'd had the rash urge to call home and see if Jenna was okay.

Closing the door, she peeked around. The foyer would have been dark but for the light that filtered through the high, arched window over the double doors. Breathing a tentative sigh, she could see that everything was as she'd left it an hour ago when she'd rushed madly from the place.

Her suitcases were exactly where she'd dropped them, in the middle of the entryway. One was toppled on its side on the white marble floor. She didn't remember stumbling over it in her haste to leave, but probably had. At that dreadful moment, she'd seen nothing in her mind's eye but the vision of her baby daughter thrashing around in a tub, drowning.

She shook her head at the memory. By now, she should know better than to call and check on Jenna while Aunt Merle and her mother, Maude, were watching "The Lusty Lunstroms." During that thirty-minute ode to lechery and greed, they were transported to the imaginary Lunstrom estate in a mythical, modern-day Sodom and Gomorrah, dubbed Goldenville, California.

Talk about bad timing! When Aly had made her I'd-better-check-on-Jenna call from the music room in the mansion, and Aunt Maude shouted, "She's drowning!" Aly had slammed down the receiver and called 911, then bolted off to save her child.

Back at the apartment, she'd found Jenna sleeping peacefully, a fire-department crew staring daggers at her, and her mother and aunt quite put out with her for her obsessive worrying.

Right in front of the 911 emergency team, Aunt Merle had reeled off a humiliating and deafening upbraiding about how Aly was *not* the only person in the world who could care for a child. Then, she'd gone on to explain that the drowning victim had been none other than prim Agathina Smatt, kindly neighbor to crafty Ricardo Lunstrom. Merle's cheeks glistened with tears as she recounted, how, if it hadn't been for the handsome vagabond strolling by, poor Agathina would be playing canasta with the fishes now.

A resigned chuckle gurgled in Aly's throat as she recalled the expressions on the faces of the two fire-department EMC men. Their humor had been badly disguised as Aunt Merle went on to reveal how—in a shocking development at the end of today's episode—the vagabond had turned out to be stalwart Lance Cane, long-lost nephew to Ricardo and recently recovered amnesiac. What good fortune, Maude and Merle had wailed in unison, that Lance was returning to his family home in Goldenville when he'd heard Agathia's shrieks for help.

Aly hoped she'd never again have reason to call 911. They'd probably ignore her pleas, anyway, since she was now on record as a troublemaking worrywart.

At least all was well with the Lunstroms for one more day. And, thank heavens, all was well with Jenna, who was safe in her crib, one finger stuck in her cherubic little mouth, looking like the angel she was.

Aly heard the sound of her self-conscious chuckle echo in the wide foyer, and was startled to see her laughing reflection in the mirrored wall opposite the doors. There hadn't been that much to laugh about lately, and the sight of her own smiling face sobered her. She ran a hand through the long, windswept stuff that passed for her hair, and grimaced at her jeans-clad image.

How out of place she looked, mirrored there beside an opulent, Louis Quinze giltwood console. A luxuriant silk-flower arrangement sat atop the gilt furniture, reproducing the entryway's color scheme of reds, golds and greens. Of course, in her profession, Aly had worked in lots of fancy homes, but this one was particularly daunting. Even when her father was alive, they'd never had a job this big. That fact probably accounted for part of her nervousness. Or maybe it was because, since her father's death three months ago, she was the major provider for her mother, her aunt and her daughter—a scary thought. Could she handle a job this huge? Or perhaps she was simply nervous because she'd made a pretty bad mistake today, and she'd vowed when she'd divorced Jack that she'd made her *last* bad mistake. From that day, she'd tried to be strong and in control.

Today, however—she'd really lost it.

She closed her eyes for a minute. Then, when she opened them, she glared sternly at herself. Enough self-recriminations. She would learn from this, and get on with her life—just as she'd learned from her disastrous marriage to Jack. She had unpacking to do, an estate to dispose of, and was woefully behind schedule.

With staunch determination, she hefted one of her heavy bags. On her earlier, aborted trip, she'd discovered that the mirrored wall opposite the entrance was banked on either side by a long, dark hallway. Behind the wall was the split staircase that curved upward to the second-floor landing. Around a bend, hidden stairs would take her up to the third floor, where the estate's lawyer had consigned rooms for herself, her mother and aunt. Heading toward the staircase, she peered down the dark hall, and froze in her tracks. A shaft of light from one of the doors sliced through the darkness. Sheer fright shot through her. *There had been no lights on earlier.*

"Oh, my Lord," she whispered in a low moan. Someone had slipped into the house after all.

Aly's first impulse was to call the police. Dropping the bag with a loud *thunk*, she spun toward the music room on her left, where she'd used the phone earlier, but before she scurried two steps, she realized her best move would be to get out of the mansion—get to safety—then call the police. Oh, no! That would mean dialing 911, she realized, and winced. Well, she simply had to do it again. She could only hope they wouldn't laugh in her face and hang up on her.

As she was about to wheel to escape, she saw a shadow loom on the shaft of lighted carpet and stilled. *Oh, Lord!* her mind screamed. *He's coming!*

Backing away in fright, she ran squarely into her other suitcase—the one she'd neglected to stumble over on her first hysterical flight out of the mansion. The old bag's untrustworthy latches flipped open on impact with the marble, coughing out a shoe, a pair of jeans, her stun gun and a tube of toothpaste.

Aly landed on all fours. The pain of the impact brought her back to rationality like a slap in the face, and she grew furious with herself. Here she was, a person determined to remain in control, and she'd spent half her day stumbling about in sheer panic! She swallowed hard. *Use your head, idiot!*

Trying to keep a lid on her fear, she scrambled to a crouched position behind the fallen luggage, grabbing for the stun gun and thanking Providence that she would at least be armed for the confrontation. She hated not being in control of her life, and this victim thing—this violent-crime business—was the pits! Clutching the stun gun, she tried to think what her favorite murder-mystery heroine, Jessica Fletcher, would do.

Before she could come up with a scenario, a wide-shouldered figure ambled out of the lit doorway. Aly gulped, her eyes going wide. To ease her anxiety, she tried to assure herself. *Jessica would probably gulp!*

Aly had never seen a criminal before, let alone one in the act of thievery. A worrisome thought niggled at her brain. For a criminal hell-bent on robbery, he was decidedly empty-handed.

As a matter of fact, he looked more like he was undressing. He was actually unbuttoning his shirt. Sensual, pouty, yet all-male lips were clamped around a cigarette, and his clefted jaw was shadowed by stubble. His thick hair was black, tousled, and curled about the upturned collar of a rumpled shirt.

Deep-set dark eyes were aimed directly at her. And why not? Who wouldn't take time out of their busy schedule of robbing a house to notice a crouched woman wielding a stun gun?

He halted at the entrance to the grand foyer and stared down at her. It upset Aly to note that he continued to unbutton his shirt. His chest, wide and swathed with a mat of hair, flaunted a brawny immodesty.

Oh, no! she cried mentally, having a sudden, ghastly thought. *Could this unshaven, brooding beast be a rapist? What have I walked into, here?*

She pulled the suitcase close to her as a barricade, but because it was unlatched, she succeeded only in causing it to fall open, the opposite side slamming loudly against the marble. She paled. He must think she was offering him a change of clothes, since he seemed to dislike his shirt so much.

Aly's brain shrieked, *Don't be such a wuss. Jessica would be spunky and face him!* Aly wanted to shriek back for her brain to mind its own business, but she was too occupied watching this smirking hoodlum step across the first bag she'd dropped, as he headed toward her.

Facing the fact that a person who wanted to be in control of her own life must *take charge,* Aly lifted her stun gun in a threatening manner—at least she hoped it was threatening. For once, she thanked heaven for the home-shopping channel—the second of her mother and Aunt Merle's two major vices.

Aly's mother had bought the stun gun weeks ago for her daughter, but Aly had never even read the instructions on how to operate it. For all she knew, if she pressed any buttons, she'd zap the pudding out of herself and charbroil her spleen! "You—you take that shirt off and I'll use this!" she warned, immediately dissatisfied with the lack of conviction in her tone.

His hands stilled on the final button of his shirt. Looking almost bored, the mugger/rapist, sucked in a long drag on his cigarette and blew out a thin stream of smoke, muttering, "Kinky, sweetheart."

Her firm expression mutated to one of frightened perplexity. If he'd said, "I don't care, I want you, baby," she'd have known what to do. She'd have zapped him, or at least tried. If he'd said, "Okay, I give up. You remind me too much of spunky Jessica Fletcher," she'd have held him at bay while she called the police. But how was a person to react to "Kinky, sweetheart"? His impassive expression didn't make sense.

While she hesitated, he took a step toward her. Having undone the last button, he shrugged the shirt off his shoulders and allowed it to flutter to the marble at his feet.

"I mean it, I'll use this!" she cried, scrambling backward in a half squat. Her mind berated her for squatting. Brave people who were in control didn't squat — at least, she'd certainly never seen Jessica doing any crab imitations.

The dark marauder eyed her a moment, looking massive and wicked; then, with his teeth clamped on the cigarette, he grinned. It was a sarcastic expression, yet there was something so sensual about that show of teeth, Aly shivered.

"Lady," he began dryly, "if you're trying to turn me on with some twisted sex game, check me tomorrow. All I want right now is some sleep."

"Sleep..." she echoed in disbelief. So that was it! He was a homeless person looking for a dry, cool place to spend the night. Wichita did get hot in August. She eased her stun gun down slightly, still not sure if she should trust him. "I—er—there are places people like you can go," she tried.

His grin faltered. "If you mean hell, I've been there."

She pushed herself up to stand, and it bothered her quite a bit to realize that even at her full five-feet-seven, he still towered a good eight inches above her. "No.

There are shelters for—homeless people. Let me, er, call someone...."

He frowned, then took the cigarette butt from between his lips and dropped it on the marble, crushing it with his loafered foot. Aly noticed he wasn't wearing socks, and his jeans were frayed and worn. Another shiver raced through her. This tall, half-clad man seemed to be awfully well-preserved for a derelict. The rapist theory reared its ugly head again.

"You—you really should have more respect for, uh, property..." She continued to back away, reviving her plan to escape. Sometimes getting out of a bad situation was the best way to remain in control. She's learned that lesson well, living with Jack. Motioning with her stun gun, she said, "I—think you'd better just go—"

He crossed muscular arms before his naked chest. "Oh, you do?"

She felt around for the doorknob behind her back. One more instant, and she'd be out, scrambling wildly away, hightailing it for the first police car she could attract—if she gunned her old pickup truck, maybe it would chug and cough to over fifty-five miles per hour and actually break the speed limit.

She only hoped she could get it moving fast enough by the time she passed the doughnut shop to attract a patrolman's attention! She turned the knob. It rattled—a dead giveaway that she wanted to leave. Trying to keep her face from reflecting her fear, she kept turning; the knob kept rattling. *Rats! Stuck!* She'd have to turn around and yank for all she was worth, and this disreputable stranger could reach her in only a couple of big strides if he had a mind to. Unfortunately, he didn't look dumb. Who knew if she could get away before he grasped the obvious—that she was making a rather futile escape attempt?

She assumed a pleasant expression. "Yes. I think you should go. You—see—" she pulled on the knob, masking the rattle with her words "—I'm in charge here."

"Are you quite sure of that?"

His cobalt gaze was direct, assessing, and Aly thought she heard a touch of irony in his tone. He knew who was in charge, and she was fairly sure he didn't believe it was Aly Fields. She only wished she didn't agree with him. She was about as much in charge as a piece of Cheddar cornered by a hungry rat. Boy, did she hate this! And she hated this man for trying to make her a victim. Well, he wasn't going to succeed. She coughed to hide another rattle at her back.

"Apparently it's stuck," he offered, his expression darkly wry.

"What's stuck?" she asked, faking confusion to buy time.

"The door. And don't ask me what door. The door you're trying to get open without my knowing," he explained matter-of-factly, drawing one step closer.

Fully aware that time was growing short for any escape, she aimed her stun gun forward, stiff-armed. "This will render you helpless, buster," she challenged. "I'd advise you to keep away from me."

Aly had never understood how frightening a grin could be, but when this unshaven intruder grinned in such an insolent manner, she felt her legs go weak. He was obviously lust-crazed and fearless. Maybe he was on some mind-altering drug. Frightened to the point of light-headedness, she cried, "What's with you? Are you high on PMS or something?"

"I think you mean, PCP," he corrected. "And the answer is no."

"Haven't you ever seen a stun gun before?" she demanded, sounding like Minny Mouse. She bit her lip. Jessica had never sounded like Minny Mouse. "Don't you know what it can do to you?" she shot back, forcing herself to lower the pitch of her voice.

"I've never seen one. No," he said with scathing amusement. "But I do know what that can do." Then he reached out, took her weapon from her, and held it up for her to see. "And I commend you for choosing the tartar-control model."

She squinted. It was a tube of toothpaste. Had she scrambled around on the floor and in her fright grabbed up the wrong thing? Of course she had. What a nincompoop she was—and what was worse, this demented, dimpled, nut case with the strong arms and hairy chest was within strangling distance—and he was now armed with her toothpaste!

Shrinking back against mutinous doors that refused to allow her to escape, she lied with false bravado, "My husband is outside—"

"Flossing his Uzi machine gun, no doubt," the stranger prompted wearily. "Look, Mrs. Fields. I know who you are and why you're here. Your suitcases in my foyer made me curious enough to call my lawyer and ask some questions."

"Your lawyer?" she mouthed in a whisper.

His brief grin held no humor. "What? You didn't know bums had lawyers?"

If there'd been a light bulb over her head, it would have lit up. "Oh, my goodness!" she moaned, appalled at her slow-wittedness. "You're the son."

"Bravo, Mrs. Fields. My lawyer tells me Mother had it written in her will that you and your staff would occupy my home until her things are auctioned."

Aly felt the blood rush from her face in her embarrassment. "Right—she knew my father in school and wanted to throw him a little business, I guess. I thought you were— Your lawyer said you were traveling."

He smiled thinly. "Charitable of him. No matter," he went on, his voice chilly. "I'm back, Mrs. Fields. And I'd planned to spend some time by myself. Your being here is damned inconvenient."

She felt a surge of self-confidence, and knew she was finally back in control. It felt good. "I appreciate your honesty, Mr. Rountree," she said, coolly. "And just for the record, your being here is rather inconvenient for me, too."

He observed her steadily, his eyes shadowed by half-lowered lids and thick lashes. "As long as we're clear. Just stay out of my way as much as possible."

She nodded stiffly, facing that intimidating stare. "My staff and I are quite professional. Don't worry about us." She could just imagine how much distress two bellowing, hard-of-hearing women and a cranky one-year-old would be to a self-absorbed, impatient bachelor.

"Well . . ." she began. "I have some more boxes and bags to carry in."

Skimming her with that contemptuous expression she was growing to abhor, he shrugged his broad shoulders. "Don't let me stop you, Mrs. Fields." Apparently dismissing her and her problems from his mind, he turned away, his agile saunter strangely taunting.

She stared, irked by his lack of manners. Rourk Rountree was a boorish, self-seeking slob, and she was going to spend the next four weeks living with him! Not really planning to do it, she shouted, "I think you should get that butt of yours off this white Italian marble, Mr. Rountree."

He slowed, then turned around. "I wouldn't concern yourself with my butt if I were you, Mrs. Fields," he drawled, his tone mocking. With a quick, wicked grin he continued on his way, leaving her to gape after him. He'd made her reprimand sound as though she had designs on the man!

That, of course, was the furthest thing from her mind. This good-looking, do-nothing slob was horribly like her ex-husband, Jack. She'd learned the hard way what a mistake it was to have anything to do with a man who was both charismatic and destructively self-indulgent. Jack had been a weak man who dreamed about striking it rich, but could never hold a job, and was domineering and controlling at home. When his dreams didn't materialize, he'd become a bitter, abusive drunk. When Aly was three months pregnant, she'd walked out, swearing she'd never be a sucker for a sexy, shiftless bum, ever again.

Mr. Rountree was exactly that. A sexy, shiftless bum. Aly didn't like the heir to the Rountree millions one bit, yet for some reason she couldn't take her eyes off him until he'd disappeared around a corner. The man was obviously jaded by life—the way Jack had been when she'd left him. And she knew exactly what this bum with the sexy walk was going to do with the money he'd get from the auction. He'd spend it on cars, trips and women, and in a few years, he'd be a sexy, shiftless, penniless, jaded bum again. Pure poison.

Aly sighed, wishing she didn't have to share his home with him for the next month. She'd heard that the aura of a family could linger in the home where they'd lived long after they were gone. But she'd never before felt it so strongly. A cloying, restrictive air hung over this mansion, and Aly wondered how a rumpled, loose-cannon type like Rourk Rountree fit into this austere picture.

Forcing her thoughts to the business at hand, she spun around and yanking on the stubborn doorknobs, she was almost upended as the heavy portals opened with mischievous ease.

ROURK LOUNGED BACK in the tufted leather chair of the second-floor library, his feet propped on the carved antique desk. Eyeing the coffered ceiling with disinterest, he took another slug of his bourbon. Damn it to blazes! He'd needed a place of refuge, and here he was, surrounded by shouting senior citizens, a screaming baby and a wild-eyed overachiever.

It had been hard to come back to Wichita, hard to face everything. He took another burning swallow, then refilled his tumbler. The booze flowed through his veins like the warm afterglow of good sex. He'd been drinking steadily for two days, working toward numb. He didn't intend to stop until he could feel absolutely nothing.

Hearing a sound, he squinted toward the library door. *Dammit!* There she was again: slender, with that witchy, liquor-colored hair always looking like she'd come in from a high wind. Of course, in Kansas, when didn't you come in from a high wind? He smiled at his private joke.

It seemed his pleasant expression gave her the courage to face him. Oh, he knew how he looked to her—like a growling, drunken beast. In the forty-eight hours little Mrs. Bean Stalk and her abusively loud batch of misfits had been there, he'd done little else but drink and snarl. "What is it now?" he shouted, not bothering with amenities.

She was holding another box. "This is marked personal, Mr. Rountree. What do you—"

"Toss it," he muttered. "I told you, if it isn't worth auctioning, toss it, Mrs. *Bean Fields*. There's nothing here I care to keep as a memento of my contented past."

"Yes, sir," she murmured, turning to go.

For some reason, he didn't like the thought of her leaving just yet. Taking another swallow, he called after her, "If this so-called security force of yours, consisting of two deaf old ladies, a baby and a slightly-built female, doesn't strike fear into the hearts of local burglars, nothing on earth will."

That got to her, Rourk could tell. Though she'd made the door, she pivoted back to face him, her mouth set in a stubborn line. Not only had she stiffened, she'd turned a glowing puce. He waited for her to blow up in his face. It didn't make any difference to him what she said, but for some reason, he wanted to be shouted at by this woman—even more than he wanted to be alone. A bitter chuckle escaped his throat. Maybe he'd finally gone over the edge. He was probably nuts, but he didn't give a flying fig—about that or anything else.

"Mr. Rountree," she began almost too quietly. "First of all, my name is Alyssa Bean Fields. I know it's odd, but I'd appreciate it if you would keep your cracks to yourself. I've heard them all. In future, just call me Aly."

He grinned and had an urge to laugh out loud. He had no idea why. She was damned good-looking when she was mad. It amused him even more to realize he resorted to the world's worst clichés when he was drunk. Restraining himself from laughing at his own stupidity, he merely drawled, "Oh, may I, Aly? You're too kind."

He could tell she was barely containing her anger. Just barely. He'd dubbed her "the control freak," and he wanted to see her lose it. Any minute now, he'd heckle her beyond her capacity to remain civil, and she'd blow.

"And secondly," she managed from between clenched jaws, "my mother, my aunt and I have never had any complaints before about our ability to offer adequate security on jobs like this."

He nodded, pursing his lips. Then he let his zinger go. "The door was unlocked when I got here—*Aly*. There are those who might find that worth complaining about."

She blinked, and he knew he'd hit a nerve. Since he hadn't mentioned her lapse until now, she must have thought it had gone unnoticed.

"That was my fault, Mr. Rountree. I apologize. It won't happen again," she stated, her face going pale.

His gut lurched. Why was he baiting this woman? Why was he so set on inflicting pain on her? She was only doing her job. Nobody was perfect. If anybody in the world knew that, he should.

Maybe because he'd inflicted so much pain on himself lately, he'd forgotten how to do anything *but* inflict pain. Taking a healthy swig of his liquor, he growled, "Just get out of here."

When she'd gone, he looked up, focusing on the empty door. From somewhere far away, he could hear Maude and Merle shouting at each other—something about cataloguing a box of silver trays. He cursed and closed his eyes. A baby began to cry, squelching his train of thought and filling his head with a new, excruciating pain—a hot, wrenching ache that seared him all the way to his heart.

A tear formed at the corner of his eye, and he wiped it away with angry dispatch. Self-pity. That's what he'd become these past six months, a self-pitying, self-hating, selfish bastard. Self, self, self. He'd been everywhere, indulged in every self-destructive act he could manage, and he was no closer to an answer, no closer to peace.

Now that he'd come back, his mother was dead of a stroke and he was having to share his home with unrelenting noise and distraction. The woman he'd just wounded emerged in his mind, and he felt a nasty stab of guilt. He was a contemptible pig, that's what he was.

With a raw blasphemy he took a stinging slug of liquor, draining his glass. "Nice going, Rountree," he muttered. Without much notice, he tapped a cigarette from his half-empty pack and put the filter to his lips. Then, in a surge of self-disgust, he crumpled the foul thing in his fist. Sagging back against the leather cushion, he closed his eyes and exhaled. "Next time, jackass, " he gritted contemptuously, "why don't you just clip her rigid little chin."

2

ALY SHIVERED, DISTRESSED by his rude dismissal. What a first-class jerk! So what if he had a point? So what if she and her elderly partners didn't make the most elite security force outside the CIA? She couldn't help it if Bean Auction was now without any men at all. Her dad had at least looked competent—big and burly—even if he'd actually been rather ineffectual. At least he'd *looked* like he could guard valuables.

She couldn't help it if a tornado had picked up his car and turned both it and her father into a front-page tragedy three months ago. But she'd be darned if she was going to whine to Rourk Rountree about her family's hard luck. She and her mother and aunt would do just fine with security. They knew how to lock up a mansion as well as anyone. Besides, there was a first-rate security system built into the house. His gibe nagged at her, though, as did everything else about him.

She sighed as she trudged along the hall, recalling Rourk's scowl. He's spent all his time these past two days either glowering at her or nursing a drink. He didn't care about anything—that was obvious. She was sure his mother would be appalled if she knew he was throwing away a century's worth of mementos, photo albums, letters; but that happened all the time in this business. She supposed she should get used to it. Some heirs simply didn't care about family history. From what she'd seen of Rourk Rountree, he not only didn't care about his family history, he didn't care much about his own future. He was committing slow suicide, wallowing in excess.

She could *almost* say she hated the man for his lack of moral fiber. Almost, but not quite. There was a recklessness about him—a sensual presence that drew her. Why she felt anything at all when he was around, annoyed her to distraction. But she did. It was almost as though he were electrically charged. She could detect a bothersome tingle at the nape of her neck when he entered a room, and she hated herself for her sensitivity to him. He was bad for her. Even worse, he was bad for himself. And he didn't give a damn about it.

Aly was hardly aware of her surroundings as she stomped away from him, her arms aching from the weight of the box he'd told her to toss. When she reached the backstairs that led to the third floor where she, her mother and aunt had been working, she began to climb, hoisting the box to rest on one hip. It seemed a waste of time and energy to take the heavy thing back. Sooner or later, the pickup they were dumping stuff in would be below one of these windows. But her sense of order prevented her from merely leaving it in the hallway. Instead, she trudged on up the stairs with the dratted box.

As she moved upward, the sound of her mother's voice calling out descriptions of silver pieces booming in her brain, her mind drifted to the question of *why* she was cursed to be attracted to n'er-do-well types. First Jack, and now Rourk Rountree. Weak, self-centered, undirected vagabonds. Well, she wouldn't make the same mistake again. Let Mr. Rountree wallow, let him shout and snarl, let him do himself in with booze and cigarettes. She was here simply to do a job. In a month that job would be nothing more than a memory. She'd be out of Rourk's life for good and all, and she could hardly wait!

When she reached the room where her mother and aunt were cataloging items, Aly went to one of the windows, set the box on its deep ledge and opened the window. Hit by a blast of stifling August air, she distractedly dropped the heavy carton outside, and it thudded into the bed of the truck piled-up with discarded goods.

After reclosing the window, she crept to the playpen and gazed down at Jenna. Just a minute ago she'd heard her crying, but now she was happily chewing on a teething toy. Aly smiled at her daughter as she gently caressed the tawny mist of hair curling about her round face. Jenna blinked up, saw her mother and held out the doughnutlike toy for an instant before she began to gum it again.

Aly noted that Aunt Merle, clad in army-surplus khaki, was perched on a cardboard box, a portable computer balanced on her knees. She was glaring at her sister.

Maude shouted across the room, "I did not call you a shrew!" Shifting her considerable bulk around from the seated position where she'd been digging into a large box, she held up a small, prism-cut bowl and bellowed, "I said *glue. Glue pot!*" Going straddle-legged on the floor, her coveralls coated with fine dust, she revealed a tarnished sterling cover and silver-handled brush. "Quit being so touchy. I've never called you a shrew. A boy-crazy flirt, yes, but not a shrew! Just catalog the glue pot."

"You're going too fast. You know I don't type on this thing as well as Aly."

"Here," Aly offered, taking the small computer from her aunt. "I'll do it. Why don't you unpack that box over there and catalog the contents in the notebook? I'll transfer it to the computer during lunch."

Merle gave up her job gladly. "You're a peach, Al, hon. I hate those newfangled gadgets. Dust makes 'em go crazy anyway. And if the rest of this floor is like this room, that computer'll be clogged up like a sink drain full of corn huskin's in half an hour."

"Have you got the glue pot?" Maude shrieked. "I'm getting a cramp."

"Got it," shouted Aly, musing that, by now, anyone within a five-mile radius probably knew the Rountrees owned a glue pot.

An hour later, Jenna was cranky and hungry, as were Merle and Maude. Besides, it was time for "The Lusty Lunstroms."

They all retreated to the gigantic kitchen where there were two of everything—two stoves, two huge refrigerators, a pantry the size of Aly's apartment, and a kitchen table that could sleep eight.

There was also a color TV with cable. As Merle and Maude huddled before the set munching on chicken sandwiches, Aly fed Jenna. A short while later, after her daughter was settled down for a nap, Aly hurriedly ate an apple and began to transcribe Merle's hen-scratchings into the computer. She shook her head. For a woman who could determine the value of a piece of jewelry within five percent of its appraised value, and in less time than most people could fall down a flight of steps, Merle's handwriting left a lot to be desired.

The Lusty Lunstroms were a bit more lusty than usual today, so Aly decided to find a less-distracting spot to work. She carried her computer down the hall, through a set of double doors, outside into the shady, gardenlike courtyard cloistered in the crook of the U-shaped house.

Ferns edged the wilderness garden, forming a lush backdrop for amethyst wisteria, snow-white azaleas, roses and shrubbery of all shapes and hues. Low, flower-blanketed ground cover hugged the bank of a man-made pond, dotted with lily pads. All but invisible among the floating greenery, peeked a few boisterous frogs, making hoarse yet restful music in the shade. Dogwood and Bradford pear trees produced a canopy overhead, their leafy branches keeping summer's cloying warmth at bay.

Past the mirrored surface of the pond and in patches among the thick stand of trees, she could see the manicured grounds, bathed in a burning midday sun.

Somehow a breeze found its way into the dense greenery, and Aly breathed deeply of the sweet, earthy scents. A stone bench beside a twisted redbud beckoned, and she struck out across the flagstone patio and along the path toward it.

Thirty minutes later, sun-dappled spatters of light were drifting back and forth almost hypnotically across the computer screen and notebook as she copied the information onto her hard disk. Birds chirped in the branches above her, and Aly began to succumb to nature's subtle lullaby. It had been a long time since she'd relaxed in a tranquil spot during the afternoon. The urge to curl up on the bench and doze off was strong, but she fought it.

The Rountree estate was extensive, and the work to be done would require twelve-hour days, as it was. There would be no time for napping—not today, nor in the foreseeable future. She exhaled tiredly, not looking forward to returning to the seemingly endless, grimy job of cataloging.

Noting the time on her wristwatch, she was sure the Lunstroms were through conniving and scandalizing for another day. Maude and Merle were probably ready to roll up their sleeves and get to work again. Bless 'em. They were tireless, cheerful, and indispensable, and she loved them.

She only hoped she could make a go of Bean Auction now that her dad was gone. Ben Bean had been a good man, well-meaning, but not as business-wise as his wife. And being from a generation where the man was the boss, he'd headed up the auctioneering company, not always making the best decisions. So, when he'd died, they'd had a rough time. And Aly's mother, still laboring under the old-fashioned assumption she couldn't run a business, had turned the reins over to her college-graduate daughter, Aly. *Well, by heaven, Mom and Aunt Merle deserve a nest egg for their old age, and I'm bound and determined to earn them one—as well as a good life for Jenna.*

"Don't mind me," came a deep voice from the shadows beyond the pond. "I had no idea it was nap time."

She started, jerking up, not realizing she'd closed her eyes, and leaned back against the concave trunk of the redbud. Squinting across the pond, she could see a figure skulking there. That silent, lurking hulk had to be Rourk Rountree. There was no mistaking that chest. Why was the man always half dressed? He grinned, clearly content that he'd not only frightened her, but embarrassed her, as well.

Without another word, he dived into the pool, leaving almost no ripple. He'd been wearing jeans, and possibly shoes, but she wasn't sure. The man was either drunk or crazy. There was a perfectly wonderful Olympic-size pool off the west wing, and here he was, diving into a shallow pond with frogs and who knew what other slimy creatures?

He probably hit the bottom and had a concussion and was dying right this minute! She jerked the computer from her lap and put it on the bench, ready to leap to her feet and attempt a rescue—snakes and frogs aside.

Before she could, he reappeared, eliciting a startled gasp from her as he shook water from his ebony hair. "Sorry," he lied with a rakish grin, water spangling his lashes.

"What do you think you were doing?" she demanded, trying to shake off her fright. "Do you have a death wish? How deep is that pond, anyway?"

"Three feet."

"Three feet?" she repeated, incredulous. "You could have killed yourself."

His eyes were the color of midnight in the junglelike dimness of the garden. His unshaven jaw glistened blue black, emphasizing the whiteness of his teeth when he grinned up at her. "Your concern is touching, Aly, but I've been diving in this pool for over thirty years. I know what I'm doing."

"For your information, the *swimming* pool is on the other side of the house."

Lifting himself from the pond, he perched on the edge, water rivulets cascading down his contoured chest and arms. "I burn easily," he said, his tone mocking. "Sun's pretty bright about now." Dragging a jeans-clad leg up to encircle with an elbow, he added, "Don't you know it's better to stay out of the sun between ten and two?"

She pulled her feet under the bench, not wanting to chance any contact with that glistening body. And those dratted jeans were clinging to his legs and hips with an obscene disregard for modesty. She averted her gaze. "There's such a thing as sunscreen, you know. I'd suggest number thirty if you're worried about burning."

He chuckled, drawing her reluctant attention. "Since you're a perfectionist, I gather you use a sun block when you swim."

She set her mouth in annoyance. He was chiding her for being a meticulous person. To him, that was no doubt a sin. "I would use it, yes, but I don't have much free time to sin—er—swim." She allowed the blurted remark to die a mortified death. How could she have made such a suggestive slip!

Eyeing her with an easy half grin, he offered, "If you ever have any free time, I'll be glad to—" he paused, his sly look suggesting more than she cared to know about his lack of moral character "—lend you some sunscreen."

Irritated for feeling the erotic current moving between them, she pulled herself erect, retorting, "I'll let you get back to your swim."

"Actually, the swim was unplanned. It seemed like a good idea at the time."

Unsettled, she wished he was still traveling—preferably in a third-world country where there were no easy modes of transportation to Wichita. "Is that the way you plan out your whole day?" she objected. "You do what seems like a good idea at the time?"

He lifted a muscular shoulder that she couldn't help noticing was too tanned for a man supposedly afraid of burning. "Works for me," he admitted, his gaze disconcertingly direct.

"I'll bet." She stood abruptly, needing to get away. "In that case, I'll let you get back to your well-planned day. I have work to do."

She got ready to return to the house when she remembered something. Rather than have to confront him over and over by carrying down another dozen or so boxes for him to banish with a disinterested toss of his head, she decided to make quick work of the whole matter right now. Facing him, she said, "I know what you're going to say to this, but since it's my job to rid you of your unwanted possessions one way or the other, there's a roomful of boxes on the second floor I'd like your permission to either catalog or discard."

He drew up to stand before her, a dripping, sleek animal. She had the fleeting thought that he should never come out of the water wearing tight, wet jeans, unless he was with a woman he intended to make love to. The vision was lewd—but stimulating. The next obvious move would be for him to begin unbuttoning his jeans in a provocative come-on. Licking her lips, she clenched her arms about the computer, wishing she was blindfolded.

She would bet her whole commission for this job that he knew exactly what he was doing—trying to upset her, as he had been ever since they'd met. But this time, his intent was wicked, the lecherous snake! She'd had him sized up—uh, rather, figured out—that first minute she'd seen him. He was after one thing in life—his pleasure, his self-gratification—and he didn't care whom he used or humiliated to get it.

"Go on, Mrs. Fields," he prompted, his voice startling her in the prolonged silence. She flushed, suddenly aware that her mind had wandered completely away from the topic of conversation. "I—er—" Good grief! She couldn't even remember what she'd been about to say.

He tilted a brow, watching her curiously, as though he doubted her intelligence. "You were saying something about a roomful of boxes on the second floor."

"Oh, yes." She tried to appear all business. "Yes. A roomful of boxes. They're marked Pearl. I presume you want them—"

"*Hell*," he growled, cutting her off. He looked as though he'd been stomach-punched. "Toss—" He faltered, then ripping out the words impatiently, he said, "I don't know. I'll think about it."

"But," she began, knowing time was short. There was no room for indecisiveness in this business. "There's not much time—"

"Damn it, Aly. I said I'll think about it!" he spat.

Before she had time to say anything else, he'd twisted around and dived back into the pond, disappearing from view. Aly couldn't seem to uproot herself from the spot where she stood until he surfaced on the far side. With one powerful surge, he was out of the water and angrily wending his way through the foliage.

She stared toward his receding form until long after he'd disappeared. "Pearl," she murmured to the birds and frogs who dwelled in the quiet glade. "I wonder who she is?"

ROURK TOOK TWO HOURS to work up his courage to go to the second floor and to Pearl's room. He stood, framed in the doorway, his heart in his throat as memories of the place flooded back.

The first time Pearl has ever been in this room, he'd carried her there in his arms. All pink, she'd been hardly bigger than his hand. And those wide, blue eyes—the same blue as his—had stared up at him, innocent, trusting. He'd thought he would be her protector, her big strong daddy. He'd thought there would be a lifetime to get to know her. But he'd been wrong. He'd failed her, and his wife, Megan—lost them before he even knew them.

Bile rose in his throat, and he cursed roughly, reliving again the agony of hearing that they were dead, and realizing he hadn't even kissed either one of them goodbye. He'd been much too busy. The man who'd followed in his father's competent footsteps—the man in control, the young genius of the aeronautics industry—was a very busy man. He'd loved his work. He'd been good at his work. But he'd neglected his family, and now they were gone. All too suddenly and swiftly, the very busy man had nothing....

Not wanting to be there, he desperately wished he didn't have to see or remember. But he forced himself. Facing this was part of his punishment, part of the living hell his workaholic obsession to manipulate his empire, his family, had earned him.

The bedroom seemed smaller than he remembered it, and darker, though there was a wall of floor-length windows facing the tennis courts and swimming pool. The white lace curtains were gone. The furniture was gone. All the colorful storybook pictures had been removed from the yellow walls. To an outsider, the room would no longer appear to have ever belonged to a baby girl. Of course when Rourk had left, he'd demanded everything be packed away. That had been part of the reason he'd left. His mother had insisted the place remain exactly as it had been on the day Pearl died—a shrine of sorts.

He'd damned her sentimental foolishness and told her it was morbid. In truth, as he stood here now, he realized it was guilt that haunted him. It was his own culpability and grief that had made him shout and rant at his mother and made the servants cringe as he'd paced, like some dark tyrant, through the mansion's halls—day and night, night and day—a ghost of a man. Packing her things away had been just another way to try to hide from himself.

He'd tried to pull himself together, blast it—after their deaths. After all, Rountree men were unfaltering in their strength, and Rountree Aviation needed him at the helm. He'd been groomed practically from birth to take over the aircraft company. Being talented in that direction, he'd liked the work. And for six months after Megan and Pearl had died, he'd tried to take the reins again, but the attempt left a sour taste in his mouth. Every board meeting he chaired, every design change he authorized, reminded him of what he'd lost—and why.

It struck him one day, right in the middle of a luncheon meeting, that he'd *never* lived his own life. He'd been an extension of his father's ego all these years. Out of blind loyalty he'd gone along with ol' Gabe's every desire, and what had it gotten him besides anger, guilt and loneliness?

He'd thought he'd been right, thought that being the kind of leader with an iron-fist in a velvet glove had been shrewd. It had certainly made him money. But now he knew how wrong he'd been. This dominance, this kinglike control he'd wielded had alienated, then killed two innocent people who loved him.

So, in a sudden flash of clarity, that day in February, somewhere between the tomato-and-chive soup and the lamb chops à la Suisse, he'd made a tormenting discovery. As he sat there, staring down at his cooling lamb chops, he no longer saw himself as the loyal son, but as a lamb that had been led to slaughter. With nausea gnawing at his gut, he vaulted up from his chair and stalked out of the luncheon, not sure what he planned to do. Not really caring. All he knew was that whatever happened from that day forward would be his decision. If that turned out to be self-destructive, then so be it. As long as, for once, it was *his* idea!

Rourk sold the aircraft company, leaving his bewildered mother even wealthier than she already was. As for himself, he had nothing but a gaping hole where his heart should be. Directionless, he'd gone away to try to forget, to live on the edge—to die if necessary—anything to get some peace in his soul.

Rourk took a step into the room and cast an anxious gaze around. Damn it! He needed a drink. No man should have to go into a room like this—his dead little girl's room—empty, devoid of laughter, bright dreams or hopes for the future.

Unseeing, he stumbled over a box, falling to one knee. The name Pearl had been scrawled on the outside of the carton by some unknown servant. He lowered himself to the floor, without the strength to move. After a minute, the need to be near his daughter grew overpowering, and he took hold of a loose corner of tape and ripped it off. The cardboard flaps popped open, revealing a glimpse of white.

With trembling reluctance, he lifted the flap to see a snowy teddy bear. Pain slashed at his heart as he recalled the time a year ago when he'd "authorized" his secretary to buy Pearl a toy for her first birthday. He'd been far too busy for such trivia. That had been a short two weeks before she'd died. He still remembered Megan opening the box and showing the white, cuddly toy to their daughter. How Pearl had clutched the soft bear to her, and how delighted she'd been when its music box played a tune from "Beauty and the Beast."

Rourk wound the key. Almost without breathing he listened as the melody jingled and plinked to its conclusion. When the room was once again still, Rourk heard a shuddering sob and realized with horror that it had come from his own throat. The melancholy recollection brought back by the sound of that music tore at his gut—brought back every ugly recrimination he'd run away to forget. He clutched the bear to his chest as tears of remorse blurred his vision. "Pearl," he groaned, through a broken whisper. "Sweetheart, Daddy's— so—so sorry...."

AT TEN O'CLOCK, ALY AND her family decided to quit for the day. Aunt Merle had already fed a fussy Jenna and put her down for the night. After Aly had checked on her daughter and showered, she went to the kitchen to join her mother and aunt for cold tuna salad they'd made up the previous day.

She was surprised to find no one there but Rourk. He was lounging at the table, his feet propped on one end, eating a plate of the salad. When she entered he glanced up, his face revealing no particular interest one way or another. He did, however, nod toward the table, quipping, "I saved you a place."

She was hesitant. Though she didn't care much what his opinion of her might be, she was still a bit disconcerted that he should see her with her hair piled on her head, wrapped in a towel. Just because she had to moisturize her hair once a week, it was none of his business. At least her muumuu was acceptable attire—inelegant, but acceptable. Hoping she exhibited a self-assurance that shouted how unconcerned she was about his opinion, she went to the nearest refrigerator and retrieved the tuna bowl. "I thought you'd be in bed by now," she remarked, making conversation.

"Never go to bed before midnight," he said. "Tuna's good. Did you make it?"

She dished herself out a portion and replaced the bowl in the refrigerator. "No. Aunt Merle's the tuna-salad expert. But my potato salad is world renowned."

He lifted a brow, feigning awe. "Oh? That was your potato salad I heard about in Beirut?"

She almost smiled. "Probably."

"Join me?" He nodded toward a nearby chair.

She took a seat on the opposite side of the table, as far away from his sprawled form as possible. With a quick peek at him for his reaction, she noted his half grin. It bothered her that he thought her choice of seating was funny. What did he think? That she was afraid to be near him? Did he think she'd jump his bones if she got too near? What an egotistical boor. Vowing to ignore him, she plunged into eating her dinner.

"So," he began, drawing her unwilling attention, "I gather you're a snake charmer in your off-duty hours."

She stopped chewing, met his amused gaze and swallowed her bite. "What?" she asked, knowing full well he was making fun of her towel-clad head.

He got up, walked to the sink and rinsed off his plate. "What kind of snakes do you prefer?" he queried, ignoring her strangled question.

"*Jackass* eaters," she stated thinly. "If I were you, I'd sleep behind locked doors, just to be on the safe side."

He turned to face her, coolly stuffing his hands into his jeans hip pockets. Though he didn't actually smile, her remark seemed to please him. "Why, Aly, I had no idea you were so hot for me. But for the record, I never lock my bedroom door. You're welcome, anytime."

She gaped at him, mortified by his off-color suggestion. "You're quite the rutting stag, aren't you," she spat.

"We can't all make potato salad," he admitted, his features mockingly solemn. "I do what I can."

She vacillated in her anger. There were times when his dry wit got to her, and she was hard-pressed not to smile. Forcing herself, she glared at him. When she'd bolstered her righteous anger enough to speak, she charged, "I suppose you're planning to eat our food all month? That wasn't part of the deal, you know."

"I know. I've been thinking about that."

"Well," she coaxed irritably, "just how long do you expect to be here?"

Though he grinned at her, his eyes betrayed a darker emotion. "I don't know. How long does it take one to justify one's existence?" His smile became hard, his eyes cold, and he seemed to drift into another time.

Aly frowned, confused.

Snagging her gaze, again, he reverted to his devil-may-care self, suggesting, "Let's say I have groceries delivered and paid for and you and your crew do the cooking?"

She debated about asking him what his cryptic remark had meant, but decided the less she concerned herself with him the better. Instead, she reminded him, "We're not very fancy. You'd better not be a picky eater."

He perused her speculatively. "I'm not picky about much. Or hadn't you noticed?"

She had an urge to tell him a *blind bat* would have noticed, but she had the feeling that he was taunting her into doing just that. Though it was painfully obvious that he was far from picky about anything, looking at him in that rumpled cotton shirt and those torn jeans, she held her tongue.

A familiar voice caught her attention, and she turned to stare at the TV that had been playing low in the background. The set was tuned to the home-shopping channel. Aly stood and walked over to the set to listen, apprehension slithering up her spine.

The pert blonde doing the selling was chirping, "Why, hello Maude. Good to hear from you again."

"Oh, no," Aly groaned. "It's Mother."

"Merle bought a sequined sweatsuit about fifteen minutes ago," came Rourk's deep voice very near her back.

She whirled around. "She didn't!" Aly protested worriedly.

He nodded. "It'll be good for those hard-to-dress-for casual formals, or even better, those black-tie jogathons."

"You're really enjoying this, aren't you?" she retorted. Rourk was regarding her with amusement. He was too close for comfort, she could detect his scent—

whiskey and soap—and almost feel his heat. Stepping away, she found herself caught by the kitchen counter. Being so close to this unpredictable man was unsettling.

"Genuine green sequins," he was saying. "I believe it was described as a once in a lifetime deal for $89.99."

Aly watched him suspiciously. Was he really as oblivious to the tumult he was causing her nervous system as he appeared?

He indicated the screen. "I think Maude is about to purchase a short, skintight black dress."

Aly grimaced and glanced back over her shoulder in time to hear her mother's voice shout into the televised receiver, "My daughter will look wonderful in that."

"Oh, my Lord," Aly lamented under her breath.

"She's right, you know," Rourk remarked near her ear. "You'd look damn fine in that dress."

Aly twisted around to stare up at him. He was too near, invading her space, no doubt on purpose. Flustered and unhappy, she snapped, "I hate to put a crimp in your ego, Mr. Rountree. But I wouldn't give a damn to know how you think I'd look in that dress!"

His lips twitched with amusement. "What would you give?"

His insolence was unbelievable! Tight-lipped, she demanded, *"Move!* I've got to find Mother before she buys that thing!"

She shoved at him with all her might, assuming he'd make her departure difficult. She almost fell on him when he easily stepped aside. After regaining her balance, she headed toward the kitchen door. Scurrying away, she wondered which phone in this vast mansion her mother was using to purchase that spandex refugee from Madonna's wardrobe. What exactly did her mother believe to be appropriate attire for a thirty-year-old woman with an impressionable child? It was clear they needed to talk about that.

"She went that-a-way," Rourk informed her as she plowed through the door to the hall.

Abruptly Aly turned back, her towel twisting askew on her head. "Which way?"

He indicated a door on the opposite side of the kitchen. It led into the butler's quarters. "Thanks," she muttered, altering her course.

"It's too late, though. That 'Alphonse of Kansas City' original is yours for a mere twenty-nine fifty. Congratulations."

She spun to glower at the TV screen. The glib blonde was now chatting with a happy home-shopper by the name of Jamesetta. Aly groaned and sank down into a chair. "Can we cut off cable?" she croaked, rubbing her temples.

"What, and lose the Disney Channel?" Rourk teased.

"I don't need a dress. I need a college fund for Jenna," she murmured more to herself than to him. "I know Mother means well, and just wants me to be in vogue, but—"

"Wear the dress to the right bars and I guarantee you, you'll catch a rich man. Presto, college fund."

She stabbed him with a deadly look. "I can see I've made a very wholesome impression on you. Or do you think all women are tramps at heart?"

His expression closed. "Lighten up, sweetheart. It was a joke."

"Well, it's not funny. Has anyone ever told you you're twisted, Mr. Rountree?"

His nostrils flared, exhibiting his displeasure. But almost immediately he displayed his teeth in a deceptively unconcerned grin. "Twisted, Mrs. Fields? Me? Be careful with such talk, or you might turn my head." Pivoting on his heel, he strode through the nearby door to the pantry that led to the large dining hall.

She wasn't sure, but Aly thought she'd heard him mutter, "I need a drink," as he disappeared.

"Don't call me sweetheart," she protested belatedly, with an impotent shake of her fist. The only response was the squeak of the swinging door as it wagged to and fro with the force of his exit.

3

ROURK WAS OUT OF bourbon. Sitting on the edge of his bed with his head in his hands, he squinted at his clock radio. It was almost eight-thirty in the morning. No wonder he felt like he'd been run over by a bus. He'd stayed up all night and drunk up his supply of booze.

Rubbing his temples, he decided what he needed was a bit of the hair of the dog. Bleary-eyed, he sat up straight and groaned. His head felt like it was as big as a watermelon, and the marching band from hell was drilling inside. In his self-imposed agony, he grimaced, recalling that the third-floor sitting room had a bar. Pushing up to stand, he tried to ignore the percussion section thudding where his brain should be, and aimed for the stairs.

When he rounded the corner into the sitting room, he was startled to see a playpen in the middle of the floor. Inside it, clinging to the rails and rising up on wobbly legs, was a chubby baby. He frowned, squinting. He wasn't all that steady, and the sight of this tiny person made his stomach lurch with harsh memories. He'd stayed clear of babies since—

"Hellfire," he muttered, and attempted to steer his haggard and unresponsive body toward the antique bar in the distant corner. When he'd retrieved the bottle he'd come after, he headed for the door, but found himself taking an unsteady detour toward that blasted playpen and its blasted contents.

Before he realized it, Rourk was leaning heavily on the playpen's edge, scowling down at the infant. It was dressed in pink. He ground out a harsh oath. Pearl had had a frilly pink playsuit like this one.

Even though he didn't feel all that bright at the moment, he surmised that pink and ruffles were pretty hefty clues that this must be a girl baby. As he glared transfixedly down at her, she babbled, staring wide-eyed at him. It irritated Rourk to see the infant smile in his direction and gurgle happily. Didn't she know better? He hated the noisy, bothersome kid, and she was jabbering and grinning as though she thought he gave a damn.

The child's scent drifted up to him. Baby powder, but more than that, there was that indescribable, wonderful scent baby daughters gave off. He closed his eyes, trying to deny the ache that began to grow in his heart. Hadn't that cursed bourbon bath he'd been taking done any good at all? Why was he feeling such intense pain, now? He should be unconscious, contentedly oblivious! Angry at the baby for bringing back tender yearnings he'd been trying to drown, he warned, "Kid, if you know what's good for you, you'll stay out of my way."

"We'll try to remember that," came a tense, female voice.

When he blinked up to connect the remark with the face, Aly swooped into his vision, grabbing up her daughter and cradling her protectively to her breast.

Rourk straightened—at least he straightened as much as he could drunkenly straighten without falling over backward.

"Morning, Aly," he offered with a crooked grin. Then lifting the bottle for her to admire, he added, "Join me for breakfast? This bourbon is twelve years old."

"That's more than I can say for you."

He chuckled. "You're very droll for so early in the morning."

"And you're very drunk," she retorted. "My husband was a drunk, too."

She said no more, merely stood there glowering at him. Apparently she'd drawn courage from the fact that her baby was safe in her arms. It rankled him to be called a drunk. He was drunk, yes. But he was far from being a drunk. Deciding to tell her so, he crossed his arms over his chest and eyed her sternly. It was difficult, because there were two of her swaying before him. "I am not a damned drunk, Aly, my love," he defended loftily. "I may be *damned*, but I'm not a drunk."

She hiked her baby on one hip and turned away. As she headed toward the door, she charged over her shoulder, "You're spoiled and lazy." After she'd stepped into the hallway, she turned back, and with unwelcome honesty, spat, "Everybody eats dirt in their lives. The strong spit it out and survive. You, Mr. Rountree, make me sick!"

As dulled as his reactions were, it was nearly a full minute before he came up with a pithy retort. "Oh, yeah?" he stated aloud. Now there was pith if he'd ever heard it. Too bad she wasn't there to benefit by his meaty wit! He was sharp, that's what he was. Sharp and pithy—and sloshed.

It was clear that Mrs. Aly Bean Fields thought he was far from sharp, although she had deduced correctly that he had imbibed. He'd read her disdain in her narrowed brown eyes. That look had told him that, in her mind, he was worthless swill—*on his best days*. And today wasn't one of his best.

Swaying unsteadily, he gave the empty door where she'd disappeared a disjointed salute. Little Mrs. Aly Bean Fields was a bright woman. Rourk Rountree might just *be* worthless. He'd had a lot of time to stew about his life these past six months.

In all that time, he'd managed to come up with only one irritating hypothesis. Though he'd never seen himself as weak or worthless, maybe he was. Maybe what he'd called family loyalty all these years had really been a lack of backbone. Maybe he'd spent the first thirty-five years of his life never being his own man. He'd been hardworking, yes; a leader, yes; always in control, yes—at least in business. But had he been nothing more than ol' Gabe's little hand puppet all his life? Playing football in high school to gain ol' Gabe's sporadic attention. Going to Stanford to tap ol' Gabe's reserved approval. Marrying the daughter of an old crony of Gabe's, to garner his miserly affection. Becoming vice president of Rountree Aeronautics to obtain Gabie-baby's cool praise.

The litany of his past made him ground out a sacrilege for his foolish, unquestioning desire to grant his father's every wish, when he'd received so little in return. Then, with Gabe's death five years ago, he'd apparently turned into ol' Gabe. A workaholic: distant with his family and demanding at the workplace.

For the past six months, his anger and grief had sent him rampaging out of control—*his* decision. The question that nagged, though—even in his booze-fogged state—and the reason he'd come back home was: What next? Did he continue on like this until he destroyed himself? Did he want the rest of his life to be filled with constant boozing, marked by half-remembered days and mindless affairs?

Why not? He shrugged it off mentally. *As long as it's strictly my idea!* Still, some small part of him rebelled against that notion. The voice in his brain was so faint he could barely hear it. Right now, it seemed hardly worth the effort to try.

Ambling disjointedly to the door, he made it as far as the jamb, where he stopped and leaned heavily against the smooth wood. Rubbing a fist over his stubbled chin, he grimaced, recalling Aly's alarmed face when she'd grabbed up her daughter. He must look like a child molester.

Blast it, he was hurting! He was hurting so badly he couldn't hide it anymore. Not the tearing pain, not the gnawing guilt—the dirt, as Aly had called it—the damned dirt had to show up sometime, and unfortunately for little Mrs. Perfect Bean Fields, she was here to see it—*Mr. Misery. In Person. Come one, come all.*

He laughed, and the bitter sound reverberated along the hall. He elbowed his body away from the doorframe and shuffled along, going nowhere in particular. What difference did it make? He could drink himself into nothingness in one place as well as another.

As he passed the door to the guest bedroom next to the room where he'd had his chat with Aly, he peered in. The actual Mrs. Bean Stalk, herself, was standing there, almost huddling. Even in his cotton-headed state, he could tell she'd planned on hiding until he was gone.

In a sour mood, he blocked the door, staring at her. She seemed to shrink in size, and drag her baby even closer to her breast.

Leaning in, he quipped, "You know, Aly, I used to be right about everything, too." With a humorless grin, he added, "Now, I'm a dumb shit—but I'm my own dumb shit."

She watched him, wide-eyed, looking frightened, but she said nothing.

He pursed his lips. "What? No brilliant comebacks for the mean, drunken ol' child molester?"

Swallowing visibly, she whispered, "Go 'way!"

He watched her for another moment, his brain chugging along at half speed. Something pricked at his mind. Finally, what he'd been groping for came to him, and his lip curled. "Was your husband a mean drunk, Aly?" Surprising even himself, his question came out almost gently.

She paled, but didn't speak. Yet, even smashed as he was, Rourk knew the answer. Backing away, he waved a negating hand. "Hell, Aly, I may not be worth much in your eyes, but I *don't* hit mothers and babies."

She didn't appear impressed by his thick-tongued claim. He scowled at her for doubting him. Apparently his fierce image did little to reassure her, for she took a step backward.

Both contempt and sympathy mingling in his tone, he grumbled, "Okay, okay. The beast is leaving." Once he was out of earshot, he muttered under his breath, "You've eaten a little dirt yourself, haven't you, sweetheart."

Staggering along the hallway, he felt deeply ashamed for making her afraid. No wonder she hated drunks. No wonder she'd grabbed up her baby the way she had. Mrs. Aly Bean Fields had been married to one slimy bastard.

"OH, MY—OH—MY" squealed Merle.

Aly had been going through a curio cabinet cataloging a collection of Chinese pottery when she'd heard a loud crash and a scream. She'd recognized the shrill cry as coming from her aunt Merle. Merle had broken her hip two years ago, and Aly prayed she hadn't reinjured herself. Hurrying across the sitting room to her aunt's aid, she was stunned to see the portly woman on all fours, running her fingers through a pile of sparkling gems.

"Oh, my, oh, my," Merle chanted as Aly dropped down beside her and placed a comforting hand on her arm.

"Are you all right, Aunt Merle?" she cried breathlessly.

The older woman lifted a fistful of diamond necklaces, a ruby tiara and a few emerald-and-pearl odds and ends. "Look! I found these under the barrel table."

Aly noticed that the table in question had toppled on its side, and that its barrel base was hollow. Someone had hidden a fortune in jewelry within the base.

Aly picked up a double-strand black pearl bracelet with a decorative jade clasp. "This is exquisite," she breathed.

"I'd say that's worth a good fifty thousand all by itself. Fifty thousand, three hundred and twenty, to be exact. Give me a minute and I'll have this whole pile figured," Merle yelled, waking Jenna and causing her to begin to whimper.

By the time the two women had gathered up the jewels, Jenna was having a full-blown fit. Aly rushed over to the playpen and checked her daughter's diapers. Retrieving the diaper bag, she changed Jenna and turned her on her stomach, rubbing her back to soothe her.

"Somebody'd better tell Mr. Rountree what we found," shrieked Merle.

"Don't bother, Mr. Rountree knows," came a familiar, deep voice from the doorway. "I was in the room below you when the table fell. I thought someone had dropped dead, or you people were bowling up here."

Aly straightened to face her irksome host as Merle shouted, "Look, Mr. Rountree! Look at what we've found."

He peered at the sparkling gems, now piled haphazardly on a settee cushion. As he walked over to take a closer look, Aly noticed that he didn't seem as inebriated as he had that morning. At least, he wasn't weaving when he walked. He didn't look much better, but the clothes he was wearing were different. Clean, though no less wrinkled. Maybe, for some reason, he'd decided against drinking that twelve-year-old bourbon, after all.

And maybe he'd made a wrong turn somewhere, stumbling into a running shower. Naturally, when he'd stumbled back out, he would have had to change into dry clothes. By some crazy fluke, he might even have taken advantage of the pot of coffee she'd brewed. Though she hadn't made it strictly to entice him to drink it, she did have a fleeting fantasy that he'd blunder into the pot and sober up by accident.

As he picked through the pile of jewelry, Aly studied him more closely. His eyes were still red-rimmed, and the dark circles beneath them were no less visible. His face was stubbled with the same heavy growth of beard, giving him the uncouth appearance of a man who'd been on a raging binge—or perhaps, having been recently released from months of being held hostage in some dank dungeon. As she considered him, Aly thought she saw something besides the residue of drink in those darkly fringed eyes. She couldn't quite make it out. Pain, possibly? Not just hangover pain, but more—

"They were under the table?" he queried, breaking into Aly's train of thought.

"The name's Merle, Mr. Rountree. Not Mable," Aly's aunt remarked loudly, but her attention was trained on the tiara. "*Miss* Merle Meeks. I never married, you know."

Aly took over for her hard-of-hearing aunt, answering the question he'd asked. "Yes. We found them under the table. Merle's a genius where it comes to gems. She'll have their value figured in a minute."

Rourk turned his gaze on her. "I suppose this will mean another auction?"

"It wasn't because I didn't have any suitors," Merle screeched, taking up a long rope of pearls.

Rourk shouted back, "I've no doubt of that, Miss Meeks. You're quite attractive." His grin was strained, but charming.

Merle blinked up and smiled, blushing, then went quickly back to her jewelry evaluation.

Aly was startled that he'd bothered to be chivalrous. Could it be that somewhere deep within this derelict lurked a gentleman—long dormant and ailing, but not quite dead?

"Will it?" he asked sharply, drawing her back.

"What?" *Drat! She'd forgotten the question.*

"Will this confounded load of jewelry require another auction?"

"I'm afraid so. And, of course, an appraisal. Merle is amazingly gifted but she's not a jeweler." His vexation was evident. He wasn't pleased with the additional time she and her family would be intruding on his drunken slothfulness. Trying to keep her tone all-business, she explained, "It's a wonderful collection of jewelry, Mr. Rountree. To do it justice, these pieces need an entire auction of their own. I've already placed general ads in *Antiques and the Arts Weekly* and *The Antique Trader* for the auctions we're going to hold for the furniture, porcelain, and French-bisque doll collection.

"We haven't even begun cataloging for the cleanup auction that will dispose of miscellaneous items. Luckily, I have yet to do the photographing for the color brochures so I can fit these in then." She gestured in a sweeping motion with her arm, indicating the sparkling jewels on the settee. "But like it or not, for this immensely valuable collection, we'll need a supplementary brochure, more ads, and an auction on an additional day—"

"All right. Do what you have to do. Just do it as quickly as you can."

Merle cut in shrilly, "Four million, three hundred ninety-seven thousand, six hundred and twelve dollars and nineteen cents." She smirked confidently. "Give or take a nickel."

Even in her irritation at Rourk's negativism, Aly smiled at the older woman, feeling a surge of pride. "Thanks, Aunt Merle. I'll make a note." Returning her attention to Rourk, she tried to maintain an impersonal facade and not allow his impatience to upset her. "I'll get right on cataloging these. I know several collectors who'll want an opportunity to bid on most of what we've found."

"I suppose you know your business," he grumbled, picking up a woman's watch with a ruby-and-diamond band. "Mother thought this stuff had been stolen years ago."

"I wonder how it ended up here?" Aly pondered aloud.

"Who gives a damn," he intoned tiredly. "She probably hid it here herself, then forgot about it. It wouldn't be the first time." Pacing away, he paused and asked, "By the way, who made the coffee?"

Surprised by the subject change, Aly said, "I did. Why?"

"It's pretty good," he observed as he reached the door.

"I'll have a cup. Black, two sugars," chimed in Merle.

Rourk didn't stop. Didn't look back. But his sarcastic laugh echoed in the room long after he was gone.

Aly felt badly about her aunt's misunderstanding Rourk's remark about the coffee, and promised herself she'd get a cup for Merle as soon as she got a few more pieces of the jewelry cataloged. Five minutes later, however, Aly was startled to see Rourk reappear with two steaming mugs. He handed one to Merle and one to Aly. She took it, frowning in confusion. "Why'd you do this?" she asked in a whisper, wondering again about the dormant gentleman that seemed to be hiding within this scruffy bum.

His somber, bloodshot eyes met hers. "Beats the heck out of me." He sounded weary as he added, "Maybe it's my way of apologizing for this morning. I didn't mean to frighten you."

Aly's cheeks began to burn with embarrassment. "Forget it. I—"

"Your husband was an ass, wasn't he." It had been spoken earnestly and quietly, and it hadn't been a question.

Aly was stunned by his directness. *How dare he make such a damning, personal remark!* "Not that it's any of your business," she snapped, "but I loved my husband madly." She didn't reveal that the tragedy was that, no matter how much she'd loved him, Jack really *was* an ass—a charismatic, spineless, hot-tempered ass.

His disparaging glance told her he knew she was lying—at least in part. "Okay. My mistake," he muttered, dropping the subject. "Where's your mother?"

"She's down the hall, finishing up in there," Aly intoned crisply.

"Oh? I thought she might be making purchases on the home-shopping channel."

Aly's coffee cup halted an inch from her lips. "She's not, is she? She promised me—"

His perverse chuckle cut her off. "Don't be paranoid, sweetheart. I'm sure she's right where you think she is."

Aly was sitting on the floor, her portable computer in her lap. Plunking her coffee mug down on the throw rug, she eyed him grudgingly. She'd had enough of his taunting. It was evident he was paying her back for lying to him about Jack. Well, in the first place, it wasn't his business if Jack was a no-good bum or not, and secondly, she didn't plan to stand for a virtual stranger's continued badgering! Outraged, she demanded, "Did I ever tell you I hate being called 'sweetheart'—especially by someone I hardly know?"

His mouth quirked with devious allure. "Don't think so, no."

"Well, I *hate* it. It's a hollow endearment at best and a male-chauvinist put-down at worst."

"Then I should be thrashed," he suggested, mockery in his eyes.

It irked her that he was not repentant by her scolding, and she warned, "Don't ever call me sweetheart, or make any other crudely suggestive remarks to me—ever again!"

He lifted a sardonic brow. "And just what other crudely suggestive remarks have I made to you, Mrs. Bean Fields?"

"I—you—er—you're always throwing out sexual innuendoes. Like when you made that sleazy remark about that black dress. You said I'd look damn fine in it—for one thing!" She knew that was weak, but it was all she could remember at the moment. Besides, how could she tell him her worries stemmed more from the erotic way he half smiled at her or watched her from beneath lowered lashes, than from anything he said.

His cool, blue eyes took her in. "Ah, that was sleazy, saying you'd look good in a dress," he chided. "I'll try to curb my depraved, slobbering sexual insinuations in future."

"Fine!" she hissed, trying to keep her frustrated tone beneath Merle's range of hearing. With a sudden need to get away from him, she thumped the computer on the settee. The pile of jewelry bounced and slithered around as sparkling evidence of her temper. "For your information, Mr. Rountree," she retorted under her breath, "even if you employed all your best, most subtle seductive moves, you couldn't lure me out of a pit of snakes!" Vaulting to her feet, she eyed him as though he were a slime trail. "I'm not kidding. I mean every word."

He took his time standing up. When he was towering before her, he asked, "Just how much do I remind you of that husband you loved so madly?"

She felt her face drain of heat.

His stare was irritated, assessing her openly as he said, "There's something about me that reminds you of him—attracts you—and you hate yourself for that attraction. Right?"

He paused, but she could only blink, wide-eyed. After a tense moment, not improved by Merle's loud, off-key humming as she worked, he went on, "Do I dare assume that you two had little else between you but a hot sex-life, and you miss that? I'm right, aren't I?"

Tongue-tied, she couldn't speak. She could only stare. Her whole being seemed to be filled with waiting. Even as inelegant as he was, standing there in torn jeans and a rumpled, half-buttoned shirt, he was compelling, his magnetism devilishly potent. *Right!* her mind cried. *You do remind me of him—we did have a hot sex-life! And I hate myself for being drawn to you!*

His expression hardened, and his eyes suddenly held a burning, faraway look. It was almost as though he'd read her thoughts and was disturbed by them. "You'll learn to hate me," he growled. "Believe me, I have." He grinned, then, but it was an ill-humored, bitter expression. "You see, I've been busy for some time now, doing myself damage. Gratuitous sex, booze—you name it, I abused it. Rourk Rountree's a great guy to avoid—take it from a drunk who knows. However, Mrs. Bean Fields, if you find yourself crawling out of your happy pit of snakes and into my bed—because I remind you of your dead, madly-loved, husband—don't count on me to kick you out. I don't have the backbone to be gallant." Pivoting away, he broke their intense eye contact and freed her will.

She sucked in a harsh breath, fighting the need to sink to her knees. He was so disturbing to her in every way that she could do little more than stutter angrily, attempting to form a stinging retort. "You're an egotistical jerk!" she finally managed in a hoarse whisper. "No— No, you're a pig!" She was desperate to prove to him that he was nothing to her—that his suspicions were completely wrong. And they were wrong. They were! She could never be attracted by another good-looking, do-nothing drunk. She'd promised herself . . .

Undeterred by her stammering rage, he called through bitter laughter, "That's right, sweetheart. You're learning." Then, he was gone.

Aly had been mistaken earlier. There was not one atom of gentleman lurking in him. She'd no doubt hallucinated the whole thing. Probably breathed in too much dust. He was nothing but a self-serving devil, through and through.

"Aly?" Merle called in what, for her, was probably meant to be a whisper.

She twisted around to see her aunt sitting cross-legged beside the bottom drawer of a dresser. "What, Aunt Merle?" she croaked, her voice strangled with anger.

"Where's he going?"

"To Hades, I hope!"

Merle looked startled. "To watch a soap? Which one?"

"My guess would be, 'The Drunk and the Smutty'!" Aly observed defiantly, still fighting her emotional upheaval.

With a quick smile, Merle turned back to her work, "I used to watch that one, until evil Angelique Potspepper got decapitated when that out-of-control airliner taxied into her wig boutique." She shook her head, bellowing over her shoulder, "I'm surprised Mr. Rountree would keep watching that show. I've heard this past season's been stuffed full of gratuitous sex."

"Bingo . . ." Aly mused, feeling her heart plummet to her feet. Without knowing it, Aunt Merle had hit upon Rourk's main thrust in life. She groaned at her word choice. But it was true: Booze and gratuitous sex were the hallmarks of Rourk's existence. He'd said so, himself. She loathed him; the very sight of him made her want to run, screaming, in the opposite direction.

As she sank back to the rug, anger surged in her, more at herself now, than at Rourk. She did loath him! She was not attracted to him at all. *But,* her mind jeered, *there is something boldly stirring in his craggy face, in his dark, cynical glance.*

There did seem to be a nobleness about him that tugged at her heart at rare, unexpected times. He was very like the miscellaneous boxed lots of items they sold at auction. Flats filled with odd dishes, old bottles or bric-a-brac—mainly junk. But, sometimes a lucky buyer was rewarded for her blind faith by hidden treasures—gold among the dross. Some dratted voice inside her kept nagging that she must dig for that gold, that unknown treasure beneath the physical wreckage of Rourk Rountree.

Early on, she'd found something endearing about Jack, too. She supposed she never would forget the first time she'd seen him riding broncs at the local rodeo. He'd been a pretty good bronc rider, and he'd looked so sexy sitting up there astride the fence when he'd turned her head with, "Hi, pretty lady." So blond and tanned and sure of himself, she'd fallen in love right then.

She'd been nineteen, and he'd seemed so mature and masculine at twenty-seven—with such a seductive smile. They'd gotten married two months later—about the time his riding went to hell and he started breaking bones. She'd gone to college and worked for her dad while Jack followed the rodeo circuit. When he couldn't ride anymore, he quit. Restless and unhappy, he'd started sinking what little money he had left into a succession of get-rich-quick schemes, until he was deep in debt. The glamour of the rodeo gone, and the dream of instant wealth fading, Jack stayed out drinking until all hours, blaming Aly and their marriage for his problems. Jack had always visualized himself as wealthy and famous. He didn't have the strength of character to get a regular, unglamorous job and be an average guy.

He quit even trying to work, and lived off Aly's share of the auction business. The day finally came when he'd become so sick of himself and his life that he started using his fists on her. She ran a shaky hand through her hair at the memory. "You're stupid, stupid, stupid . . ." she muttered between gritted teeth, trying to cast aside any soft notions about Rourk Rountree. "Don't get involved with him! No matter what you might think you see—or *want* to see—don't waste your time looking for gold that isn't there. He's just as weak as Jack was, and that's poison for you."

AT ELEVEN O'CLOCK THAT night it was dark and pleasantly cool outside on the patio. Jenna was sleeping soundly, for Aly had just checked on her. But for some reason, she couldn't even consider going to bed, yet. She was wide-awake and as jumpy as a cat in a hailstorm.

She hadn't seen Rourk since the incident with the coffee, twelve hours ago. She certainly hadn't been disappointed when he wasn't in the kitchen when she and her aunt and mother had eaten cold meat loaf sandwiches for dinner.

Walking out into the starlit night, she sighed, trying to convince herself that she didn't care if he was drinking himself into a stupor somewhere. In the distance she could hear the mellow croak of frogs, and the *thit-thit-thit* of the lawn sprinkler system as it made its mechanical rounds.

A breeze teased her hair and ruffled her knit top, and she breathed deeply of the cool, grassy scent of the August night. Her spirit calmed somewhat, she headed toward one of the cushioned patio chairs.

Laughter caught her attention, and she perked up her ears. Her aunt's voice came to her from a distance, amid a chuckle, "Today I found a 1920 sex manual, Maudie. I couldn't believe what I read. It said how the man should prepare the woman for sex."

Maude shouted back, "Prepare the woman? How?"

"Get this. It said for the gentleman to mind his tongue and avoid vulgarities of language."

"Like what?"

"I don't know. Maybe, 'You're a hot little mama.'"

"Oh sure, in 1920? What else?"

Merle giggled. "Another suggestion was to keep smelling salts nearby to revive a maiden prone to swooning."

"Swooning! Reminds me of my first beau," Merle chortled. "Remember, Maudie? Quaxton Nitwig?"

"*Nitwit* Nitwig? Did that idiot faint when he tried to kiss you?"

"Oh, hush, you. He never quite fainted. Just got lightheaded a time or two. Nitwit—uh—Quaxton was quite a Romeo in his day—"

"Why? Because he never quite fainted? Merle, you may know a lot about jewelry, but you don't know squat about sex! You're a spinster, remember?"

"Well, just because you're a whiz at bookkeeping doesn't make you a sex expert, either. Besides, you married so young, you wouldn't know worldly things like that."

"What?" cried Maude in disbelief. "Ben, rest his wonderful soul, knew how to prepare a woman like no man in the world!"

"Oh? Did you ever go to a double-feature drive-in with Waymon Drope?"

"I wouldn't go to a hog-calling with Waymon. He had a snout like Dumbo. Why, you couldn't get near enough to kiss him with such a smeller!"

"Waymon's smell—uh—nose was very sexy!" protested Merle. "And you know what they say about big noses...."

Aly smiled and shook her head, deciding she'd better go back inside. This conversation wasn't meant for anyone else's ears. When she turned to go, she slammed into the hardest chest she'd ever run into—with her face, that is. Grimacing, she recognized, even in the moon-bathed darkness, that expanse of chest, and detected the scent of the man she had come to know and wanted to avoid with a passion. And once again, he was parading around half-naked.

Arms surrounded her to keep her from stumbling backward. When she'd righted herself, she whispered harshly, "You may let me go, now."

"May I?" Gathering her even more firmly in his arms, he held on, taunting, "And I thought you were attempting a rather clumsy come-on."

Unwillingly, she was molded into the contours of his lean body. The warmth of his arms, his bare chest, was so bracing, it was hard for her to react appropriately. Her mind was demanding that she push away, but her body sagged into him, suddenly unresisting.

His touch, firm and persuasive, invited more. She cursed her paralyzed limbs. Her traitorous arms! Her back-stabbing, rubbery knees! Gulping several times, she tried to coax her voice to come to her aid. Nothing happened.

"I'll have you know," Merle went on loudly, "that I lost my virginity at fifteen."

"You lie!"

"Out by the duck pond with Harmon Dowripple."

"Merle! Harmon Dowripple went into the priesthood."

"Because I wouldn't run away with him."

Rourk chuckled softly. "Sounds as though you come from very sexy stock." His breath, soft against her hair, made her catch her breath.

She forced her gaze upward to meet his. At least she could get her head to move. That was something. But, when she saw the laughter in his eyes, she cursed her body's ability to pick and choose its area of infirmity. She wished she hadn't been able to witness the clear-cut lines of his face, those inviting, teasing lips.

She had no desire to back out of his embrace, and that frightened her more than the lure of his moonlit features. His breath, moist against her forehead, sent a shiver of anticipation through her. Was he planning to kiss her? Did she see erotic resolve in his gaze?

She mustn't allow it—not in her irrational state. She must find a way, not only to make her escape—unscathed—but to make him lose interest in her as a sexual being. *If there was any gold in this man, she would eat her computer!* Her new rule, as far as men went, was that they had to be solid, hardworking citizens, and really deserve her passion before she would give it!

Aly's mind cast about for a plausible argument. As she floundered, her body insisted on registering the taut maleness of him. Half conscious of Merle and Maude's running conversation, she caught on her aunt's bellowed comment, "I'll have you know I could have written that movie with Marlon Brando. You know, *Last Tango in*—er— What's it?"

"*Last Tango in What's it*," Rourk repeated through low laughter Aly could feel in her breasts. "I must have missed that one."

Disgusted with herself for her frailty, and put out with this man for eavesdropping on her mother and aunt, though their shouting had no doubt alerted neighbors a mile away as to their sexual exploits, she forced herself to remember who Rourk was; what he was—a lazy, good-for-nothing, boozing egomaniac looking for a quick roll in the sheets. With that raunchy vision entrenched in her mind, she forced his arms away. "For your information, Mr. Rountree," she rasped, "you're going to miss *this* one, too. Now, if you'll excuse me."

She sidestepped around his considerable bulk and headed for the door. "By the way, my family's sexiness is none of your business, but I'd wager you spring from a long line of sex-manual cripples."

The mellow laughter that chased her from the patio was deep and amused. Such an unkind slash at a man's ego should have at least given him a few seconds of unease! It was obvious that Rourk Rountree was not concerned about any problems with his sexual prowess.

This new knowledge both aggravated and intrigued her, and she berated herself for her curiosity. His bedroom expertise was none of her business. None! Zero!

¡Nada! The glass patio-door panels rattled with her furious slam as she ran away down the hall.

She despised Rourk Rountree and she planned to continue to despise him. Balling her fists with harsh determination, she renewed her vow not to find a single attractive quality about another, charming bum! No matter how tempting he seemed in the moonlight, no matter how taut and inviting his arms might feel, she couldn't be that flawed, that foolish. Not again. She couldn't allow herself to be—or there'd be the devil to pay!

4

ROURK STARED UP AT THE coffered ceiling of the second-floor library and took a sip of bourbon. Recrossing his ankles on the padded desktop, he wondered aloud, "What is it, Rountree? Misery loves company? Why are you giving that woman so much grief?"

He practically insists she go to hell one minute, then comes on to her the next. *What's the point?* Taking a hefty swig, he emptied the glass, lowering it to the desk.

Abruptly he stood and went over to the leaded windows that overlooked the garden. It was nearly seven o'clock and the sun was blocked by the west wing of the house, placing the leafy retreat in deep shade. Aly was out there, sitting rather stiffly on a patio chair, entering something into her laptop computer. He smiled, but it wasn't due to any measurable degree of happiness. More a resigned expression. The young Mrs. Fields, he noticed, never took a break. She worked, hardly ate; worked, hardly slept; and worked—hardly smiled, now that he thought about it.

So, why did he insist on making her life that much more miserable? Maybe that's what directionless slobs did all day—make other people's lives miserable. Maybe that was the way directionless slobs felt superior, making other people feel rotten. He didn't know. He hadn't been a directionless slob long enough to be sure of all the rules. He snorted wryly, noting his backsliding into his old way of thinking. No doubt, directionless slobism had no hard-and-fast rules. That lack of rules, he supposed, was the very point of being a directionless slob in the first place.

He leaned against the cool panes, a troublesome thought dogging his brain. It had been bothering him ever since last night when he'd almost kissed her out there on that patio. What the hell had been in his twisted mind?

Was it because she had her head on straight and he didn't? Maybe she was too straight. Maybe she needed a little loosening up. Maybe he itched to do the loosening.

There was such a thing as being too driven for perfection. The process sucked up your life and left you nothing but a shell. From what he'd seen of Aly, she was driving herself like a freight train toward a washed-out bridge. He laughed. The sound was short, rough and biting. She reminded him of himself six months ago, a year ago, five years ago, twenty years ago....

Rourk had had to be perfect, to be a leader, to get his father to notice him. He wondered why Aly had to be perfect. Why she had to be in tight control of her world. Last night, he hadn't been all that sober. Maybe he'd thought if he kissed her he'd help in some weird way— by osmosis, siphon off some of her overperfection gene, and thereby give her a chance to miss the headlong tumble into the gorge like the one he'd taken.

He shook his head. Whatever he'd thought, it was 100-proof stupid. Even if he'd just wanted to feel her lips against his, it was stupid. She obviously didn't want a drunk hanging around her. She had enough to deal with as it was.

Besides, he was through dictating other people's lives. If she wanted to drive herself, let her. It wasn't his business. But the idea—no, the fantasy—of kissing her, lingered. Her lips—those stern little lips—against his. He had a feeling they'd soften up quickly enough once gently prodded into submission....

To hell with her lips! Thrusting himself away from the window, he shifted back to the desk and poured another tumbler full of booze.

ROURK HEARD A THUD and then a piercing wail. He stopped dead still and listened. It must be the baby. Something had happened to the baby. Frowning he looked back over his shoulder and shouted, "Maude! Merle! Aly?"

No answer. The wailing grew more shrill.

Rourk knew it was time for the Lusty Lunstroms. Maude and Merle were probably so engrossed that even if they had one good set of ears between them, they wouldn't hear his shouts or the baby's cry.

Deciding he'd better handle it, he sprinted along the hall toward the stairs. Jenna should be in her crib taking her nap. "Aly!" he called, wondering where she'd disappeared to.

Still no response, just the ever-growing din of a baby's screams.

He catapulted himself up the steps three at a time and careened around the corner and into the room that served as Jenna's and Aly's. He was halted in midstride when he almost stumbled over the infant, hunkered down on the floor on all fours, her head craned toward the sky as she sobbed her heart out. On her forehead, a bump was growing visible.

Somehow, she'd managed to fall out of her crib. He hesitated for a minute, not knowing what to do. "Aly!"

he shouted again, but getting no answer, he instinctively swooped down and picked up the howling child.

"Don't cry, Jenna," he murmured, trying to comfort her, but knowing she must sense his inexperience. "Maybe we'd better put a cool cloth on that."

She felt like no weight at all in his arms as he carried her into the connecting bathroom. Running cold water, he sat down on the edge of the claw-footed tub and situated her on one knee. "Just a second," he said, keeping his voice low and calm. "It'll feel better."

Jenna blinked watery eyes, and let out a few more noisy squawks, but after a minute, his dark, grim face seemed to become more interesting than her head-over-heels tumble. When he'd dampened the cloth and clumsily rung it out with one hand, he placed it on the bump. "That's to keep it from turning black-and-blue," he told her, feeling like an idiot. What would a one-year-old care about first aid?

Jenna sniffled, hiccoughed, and reached out to touch his stubbled chin. At first, he avoided the tiny hand, but when she arched forward to try again, he decided it might take her mind off her head, so he let her trace her chubby fingers around his jaw.

"How does that feel?" he asked. "Better?"

She patted his chin and smiled, her rosy cheeks glistening with forgotten tears. Wriggling, she grabbed his shirtfront and made a gurgling baby noise exactly like some he'd heard Pearl make. His expression hardened, and he felt acid seep into the pit of his stomach, making him cringe at the memory.

Drawing away, he turned the cloth, placing the air-cooled side on her bump. "We should put ice on this," he murmured. "Maybe we'd better go to the kitchen."

Jenna graced him with a grin filled with four teeth, undaunted by his scowl. Waving her hand as though trying to reach his fascinating, rough chin again, she jabbered, "Dadadadadada."

"What's going on here?" a breathless voice demanded from the bathroom door. "I went to the basement for a minute and Jenna was gone."

Rourk's narrowed gaze met her fearful one. "She fell out of her crib."

Aly gasped, her eyes dropping to the remote monitor she wore clipped to her belt. "I—I didn't hear a thing." She rushed to take her child in her arms. It surprised them both when the baby clung to Rourk's shirtfront with a determined fist.

"Maybe the battery's dead," Rourk offered, disengaging himself from the baby's hold.

"No," Aly insisted. "They're fresh batteries. I make sure."

Rourk knew she was very protective. "Could be a loose wire in the main unit. I'll have a look. If I can locate a screwdriver, I'll see if I can fix it. And I'll lower the mattress so it won't happen again."

Aly paused in her worried inspection of her daughter's head to glance at him in surprise. "I— That would be nice. Thanks..."

AN HOUR LATER, the mattress was lowered and Rourk was locking the side railing into place when Aly reentered with Jenna in her arms.

"What did the doctor say?" he asked.

"She's fine. No concussion." Aly glanced at Rourk's handiwork, surprised. She'd expected his offer to fix the bed to be an empty one. She'd heard them from Jack for years. But it appeared he'd actually fixed the bed.

"I gather you found a screwdriver," she observed, trying to keep the amazement from her voice.

"Finally. Boxed up in the basement."

"Oh?" Aly said. "Maude and Merle must have packed it. I don't remember any tools. Did you—happen to find the trouble with the baby monitor?"

"A loose wire." He handed her back the remote unit. "I tested it. It works."

She took the small square unit, as once again a feeling of disbelief overtook her. "I—I appreciate it," she murmured.

"No problem." He bent to close the toolbox.

"I must admit, the crib looks sturdy enough."

"A two-year-old could have done it." He straightened with the toolbox in his fist. "I'll go repack this."

"Don't bother. I can do it," Aly insisted.

He passed her a twisted grin. "I don't doubt that, Mrs. Bean Fields. I'm sure you can do anything and everything. However, the basement's on my way. I saw a dusty old case of bourbon you people overlooked that needs rescuing."

Aly's brows knit at his baiting tone, but she didn't respond as she gently placed her tired child in the crib. She owed Rourk for his help, and didn't have the heart to quarrel with him right now. She was too grateful that Jenna was all right to be mad at anybody. "Do whatever you have to," she said wearily. "And—and thanks for helping Jenna when she fell." She faced him, tentatively. It was difficult to look him squarely in the eye. Aly hadn't thought he had a single molecule of compassion in him, and knowing he'd come to her daughter's rescue made her feel a twinge of kindness toward him. A twinge she could ill afford, considering the effect he had on her at times. "And thanks for fixing—

everything," she added almost grudgingly, clipping the remote unit to her belt.

He lifted a shoulder. "As I said, a two-year-old could have done it."

"Maybe," she admitted, averting her gaze. "But we're fresh out of two-year-olds."

There was a long pause, then, "Yeah— I know...."

His tone held a note of bitterness. Curious, she lifted her regard. When their glances locked, his features altered, and she had the feeling the sneer he aimed her way was there to mask some darker emotion. "Mrs. Bean Stalk," he quipped perversely, "in future, try not to disrupt my strict agenda of self-absorbed excess with personal problems. You've put me way behind."

She stiffened, but couldn't conjure up the anger she knew he was attempting to make her feel, couldn't even be offended by his vandalism of her name. Instead, she focused on the dismal shimmer in his midnight blue eyes. "I'm sorry, Mr. Rountree," she said, sincerely. "I'll try not to disturb you again."

His smile tightened, and there was a tensing of his jaw, but he said no more, revealed no more. Abruptly, he disappeared around the corner.

Clinging to the crib railing, Aly fought a warming feeling for this inappropriate man and warned herself, "Don't soften, fool! Helping Jenna was a freak, one-time offer." Rourk was down on life, just like her worthless ex-husband Jack. And she knew firsthand what a mistake he'd been.

So the heir to the Rountree millions had helped once. So what! Forget it. He'd made it clear he didn't intend to make a habit of it.

Jenna turned on her side in her sleep and made a tiny sound of contentment that drew Aly's attention. Trying to wipe Rourk's haunted expression from her mind, she covered her daughter with a multicolored flannel sheet and went back to her work.

NOT SURE WHY HE'D DONE it, Rourk stared at his clean-shaven face in the mirror and rubbed his smooth jaw. He peered critically at himself and muttered, "Even without the beard you look like some doomed candidate for the Supreme Court *after* the what-have-you-done-in-the-past-we-can-fry-you-for hearings."

Even so, his eyes seemed clearer this morning. Clearer, but far from the eyes of a saintly man. He decided wryly he might not look as much like one of America's Ten Most Wanted criminals, but with his shaggy hair and the dark circles under his eyes, he could still hide easily among the top twenty.

Dragging on a knit shirt, he went down to the kitchen where he could smell freshly brewed coffee and home-baked coffee cake. It was rather nice to be hungry for a change. Maybe that's what one felt like when one didn't stay up all night drinking. It had been so long, he hardly remembered.

In the kitchen, Maude and Merle were bustling around, already dressed for the day, in coveralls, but nevertheless, sporting flowered aprons as they put the finishing touches on the meal.

"Well, well," Merle exclaimed. "Look who's up for breakfast! And shaved, too. What is it, Mr. Rountree, your birthday?"

He shook his head and glanced around, wondering where Aly and Jenna were. "Just got tired of the beard," he said loudly enough so that they could hear.

"You've got a nice jaw, doesn't he, Maudie?"

Rourk smiled wanly, uncomfortable with the shouted compliment. "Is the coffee ready?"

"And a noble nose," Maude added.

"Oh, for pity's sake. He didn't shave his nose," Merle shot back. Facing Rourk she said, "Coffee's ready. Would you like some?"

"I'll get it," he shouted.

Rourk had already gotten himself a mug from the cupboard and was pouring a cup when Aly entered with Jenna in her arms. "Coffee cake smells—" Seeing Rourk there startled her into speechlessness. "Great..." she finished weakly. "Good morning."

"Coffee?" Rourk asked, reaching for another mug.

"Yes. Thanks," Aly murmured, securing Jenna in her high chair.

"How many for my famous pecan-raisin coffee cake?" Maude bellowed, wielding her knife.

"Sit here," Merle told Rourk, motioning. "Aly, you sit next to him with the baby around the corner by you. Maude and I'll sit on this side."

"What about coffee cake?" Maude insisted more loudly. "Who wants any?"

"Just start cutting, Maudie. It'll get eaten," Merle ordered, dealing out plates like they were cards. "Juice, anybody? We've got tomato and orange."

When they were all seated, Aly took a sip of her coffee, surprised by Rourk's presence this morning. He'd never put in an appearance at breakfast in the week and a half they'd been there. And today, he'd even shaved. She lowered her cup and toyed with a forkful of coffee cake. He had a wonderful face, all sharp angles and planes. Masculine and, ironically, strong looking. The cleft in his chin was more pronounced without the dusky growth of beard, and his eyes seemed darker, more intense by comparison. Or was it because he seemed completely sober today?

She'd only allowed herself a brief glimpse of him before she sat down, but that glimpse was stamped forcefully on her memory, refusing to be relegated to a corner of her brain reserved for unimportant matters.

"Don't you think Mr. Rountree looks nice today?" Merle asked Aly.

Choking on the bite she'd just taken, Aly doubled over in a fit of coughing, discovering after a moment that Rourk was helpfully patting her back.

"Are you all right?" he asked, sounding amused.

She nodded disjointedly, lunging for a glass of water. When she'd had a few sips and regained her ability to breathe, she lied, "Pecan went down the wrong way." A brief peek at Rourk told her he knew exactly why she'd choked. He didn't appear overtly jolly, but he did seem aware of Merle's intent, and his narrowed eyes betrayed a mocking twinkle. Aly promised herself to talk to her aunt about her matchmaking tendencies. They were all-too-transparent to everyone concerned.

"As I was saying, Aly," Merle began again, "don't you think Mr. Rountree—"

"Well," Rourk interrupted, coming to his feet. "It was a wonderful breakfast, ladies. But I think I'll be going." He cast a taunting glance at Aly, adding too quietly for either Maude or Merle to catch, "This might be a good time to tell them you wouldn't have me if I were the last shiftless bum on earth."

She lifted mortified eyes in time to see his devil-may-care flash of teeth. As he strolled away, Merle shouted, "What? I couldn't hear that."

Rourk's biting laughter reverberating in the hall, Aly whispered loudly, "Aunt Merle, it doesn't matter what he said. The gist of his remark was, that he's—er—not my type. And that echoes my sentiments, exactly. Understand?"

Merle made an impatient face. "I just said he looked nice. Make a federal case!"

Maude interjected, "You're as subtle as a hound dog chewing up somebody's backside. Leave the children be."

"But they're so cute together."

"We aren't cute together," Aly retorted, upset. "We're strangers who have nothing in common. Period."

Merle shrugged, scooping out another slice of coffee cake. "Okay. Who am I to talk—a spinster and all?"

Aly was suspicious of her aunt's perfunctory tone. She'd given up too easily. "Aunt Merle, I mean it. No more 'Isn't he attractive?' comments."

"Tick-a-lock," Merle promised archly, her fingers twisting at her mouth as though she were turning a key. "My lips are sealed." She peered at Aly, warning, "But mark my words. He's a nice-looking boy. You could do worse."

"Jack was nice looking, too," she reminded, unhappily.

"Jack was a *bum!*" both Merle and Maude shouted in unison.

"So is—"

Aly's exasperated reply was cut short when Jenna knocked her cereal bowl to the floor. Seconds later, Aly was relieved to find herself on her knees mopping up the goop, as Merle and Maude switched topics to the dirty job that stretched ahead of them that day: unpacking boxes in the extensive attic.

As Aly scrubbed the wood planks clean, she prayed the subject of Rourk Rountree's attractiveness would not come up again.

MRS. HELENA ST. ALBYN Rountree's bedroom was an auctioneer's nightmare. There must have been forty oil paintings on her walls, a thousand crystal, pottery and china collectibles crammed onto every available flat surface. A closet was packed with seventy years' worth of clothes and shoes. All shapes and sizes of quaint throw rugs adorned the oak floor. Drawers were awash with odds and ends of semiprecious baubles, personal items and junk.

A fine coat of dust covered everything visible. Aly sneezed, the act making her cringe with the ache that had begun in her back from lifting heavy pictures off the wall and then stooping to dust them. She'd removed and cleaned twenty that morning, lunch was over, and Jenna was fast asleep upstairs in her crib.

With a weary sigh, Aly leaned across a damask settee and grabbed a murky oil painting of what appeared to be either a blue hell or a hurricane wreaking havoc somewhere out on the ocean. Though it wasn't Aly's idea of pleasing art, she knew a V. T. Snodgrass could be worth as much as twenty thousand dollars at auction, and the woman's signature was swirled in the lower right-hand corner of this stormy purgatory.

With her knee on the settee, Aly juggled the artwork down to rest it on her thigh in order to get a better hold. Glancing at the wall, her eyes chanced on the most disgusting sight she'd ever seen. In a knee-jerk reaction, she let out a piercing scream, dropped the painting and spun around to escape.

In blind panic, she tore from the room and crashed into a solid object—an object that was warm, clothed, and expelled an exceedingly masculine "Woof" upon impact.

Still seeing in her mind's eye the awful sight in the bedroom, she wailed, "Gross! Gross! Gross! *Yuck!*" Pressing to her substantial haven, a shiver of aversion swept through her and she threw her arms around her protector's neck, holding on to him with all her might.

"What is it?" Rourk asked, grasping her gently but firmly.

She swallowed and shook her head, shivering again.

"Aly," he pressed, "are you hurt?"

She held on nuzzling ever so slightly as a feeling of comfort, of being protected washed over her. She liked his scent. It was different than before—no hint of booze, but a heady mixture of sandalwood and cedar. And his body was warm, huge, encompassing. How long had it been since she'd felt comforted? How nice it felt to be held in someone's arms again. How nice it would feel to be able to relinquish her rigid self-control, and to know her trust wouldn't be abused once her guard was down. She inhaled him, held him and closed her eyes, wishing . . .

"Aly?" he queried again. "Are you all right?"

His concerned question brought her back to where she was and why. That cold splash of reality filled her with the niggling feeling that she'd made a big, fat fool of herself. People in control didn't make fools of themselves over such trifling, childhood fears. Trying to regain her composure, she lifted an embarrassed gaze to scan his face.

Boldly handsome, but with his features drawn in worry, he was watching her. She felt stupid, and snaked her arms from around his neck, murmuring, "I—I'm okay. It was just a—" even the thought of it made her body shudder as she finished "—a spider."

His expression changed, and there appeared signs of humor about his mouth and his eyes. "All this over a spider?" he asked gently.

His amused tone pricked her pride. "Well, for your information, it wasn't just any spider. It was a spider you'd hire to do heavy lifting. It was huge," she cried defensively.

He grinned at her, and the melting effect it had on her legs was troublesome. She backed away, but was stalled as his arms wound about her waist.

"Would you like me to kill it for you?" he asked teasingly.

"I'd like you to let go of me, actually."

He arched a brow. "Are you sure you're through climbing on me?"

Her cheeks went hot. *How lewd!* "When I decide to climb on you, you'll know it!" she shot back.

Wicked humor glittered in his eyes, and his smile broadened a notch. Aly was aghast to realize what she'd said and backpedaled, "I— What I meant was, I'll let you know when I intend to climb on—er—I'll climb on you when—" Heaving an angry groan, she cut herself off. He hadn't said a word, just stood there grinning like a horny baboon, letting her dig her own grave. More incensed with herself than with him—but not by much—she shoved his arms away.

Needing to wipe away that damnable smirk of his, she decided to strike fear into his black heart, charging, "There are those who'd call this sexual harassment, you know!"

"Yes," he agreed, still grinning. "And I'll thank you to keep a civil tongue in your head."

"Me?" she cried, amazed at his gall. "Oh, you're very droll. Someday there'll be a bust of you in the Funny Man's Hall of Bums." Spinning away, she marched back into the master bedroom.

Avoiding the spot on the wall where the mammoth squashed spider clung, she found herself squirming about how she was going to remove the paintings nearest to the eight-legged carcass.

"Where is this beast of yours?" Rourk asked at her back, startling her into a yelp of surprise.

The "beast" in question—a big, brown blot about six inches in diameter, with legs—was all-too-obvious against the beige silk wallpaper.

"It's dead," he remarked almost to himself.

"I know it's dead," she hissed. "I simply didn't expect to see a giant spider's corpse smutched all over the wall. Call me nutty for not snapping its picture and sending it to the *National Tattler* with the caption, Despondent Arachnid Commits Suicide By Bludgeoning Itself With Oil Painting From Hell."

An ironic smile tugged at the corner of his mouth. "That's pretty cute. You can be amusing company when you try."

"You're absolutely *infested* with charm aren't you?" she snapped.

"Absolutely," he drawled, eyeing her with interest. "Just out of curiosity, what exactly does 'smutched' mean?"

"I, personally, think it means smudged, but chunkier," she replied shortly. "Glad you asked?"

He snorted in disgust. "Not very."

"Well, forget it ever happened. I can avoid the spider. Just go back to what you were doing and don't give the incident another thought." She flounced bravely away from him, but when she was almost to the settee where the picture had fallen, her step faltered. The *thing* hovered there like an evil spirit, haunting her peripheral vision, dogging her consciousness. She was afraid of spiders—especially big spiders. This one might be dead, but it was *big* dead, and *conspicuous* dead, and *creepy-crawly* dead.

"Mrs. Fields," came a laughter-edged voice.

"What?" she half shouted, half moaned.

"Problems?"

Aly focused away from the blob, and moved cautiously toward the framed canvas. "No! No problems," she lied, snatching up the painting and stumbling quickly away to a safe distance. That done, she faced him, clutching the ponderous abstract to her breast, and lifted a haughty chin as if to say "I am strong and in control."

Teasing laughter danced in his eyes. "It's entertaining, watching you gird your loins."

Her triumphant mood curdled and she glared at him. "Why do you insist on making everything sound so vulgar?"

He shrugged in a casual, jesting way. "Do I? Or could it be all in the way you hear it?"

His teasing manner suggested that she *preferred* reading sexual meanings into his comments. That was ridiculous! Incensed, she blurted thinly, "Don't you have a *slime trail* to leave somewhere? I wouldn't want to keep you!"

He perused her speculatively for a long moment. "Don't worry, sweetheart," he finally offered, his expression turning serious. "I won't tell anybody you lost it because of a dead spider. Your secret's safe with me." Tapping his forehead in a mock salute, he shifted around and soundlessly left the room.

She gaped after him, feeling her face drain of blood. Could his snide accusation be true? Could she have lashed out at him because she was upset with herself for her irrational hysteria over a dead spider?

She closed her eyes and exhaled unhappily. Of course. Even she could see that now. For a shiftless bum, the man was distressingly perceptive. Aly was ashamed that anyone—especially Rourk Rountree— had witnessed her failing, and she'd taken her anger out on him.

When she finally found her voice, he was long gone. Yearning to make an assertion in her defense, however weak, she gritted, "I—I told you before: Don't call me sweetheart. . . ." It came out sounding unbearably forlorn.

5

ALY HAD CALMED DOWN considerably since yesterday's squabble with Rourk. She was sorry to have to admit it, but it wasn't just her coolheadedness that had turned the tide. It was, in part, when she'd taken thirty minutes off yesterday afternoon to check on Jenna and feed her a snack, she'd come back to find the spider removed from the wallpaper.

Rourk had to have been the one who'd removed it. No one else had even known. Just why he'd cleaned the wall, she had no idea. Maybe the notion of a squashed spider in his beloved mother's bedroom bothered him. Maybe he'd thought it would reduce the selling price of the mansion—he'd only get eleven million nine hundred and ninety-nine thousand instead of twelve million. Who knew? But, the spider was gone, and she was grateful.

She hadn't seen Rourk the rest of that day. It appeared he was avoiding her. Or, perhaps he'd locked himself in his room so he could wallow in a drunken stupor. Whatever the reason, she hadn't seen him. She didn't look forward to spotting him, however, because she had an antsy feeling she ought to say thank-you. And having to show gratitude to a weaving, jeering drunk was not her idea of a rollicking time.

She checked her watch. It was past noon. Jenna would be waking up fussy and hungry any minute. Wiping her hands on a towel, Aly quit washing Mrs.

Rountree's bric-a-brac in the huge tub adjoining her room, and headed along the hall to Rourk's study where Maude and Merle had been boxing a variety of collectibles in preparation for washing.

When she rounded the corner she was startled to see the heir to the Rountree fortune bent over his desk amid a disarray of papers, with Jenna cooing happily on her back in front of him.

She halted, apprehensive. "What do you think you're doing?" she asked sharply.

Rourk glanced over at her, his features drawn in a scowl. "Ah, finally. Why didn't you answer me when I called you on that monitor?"

Instinctively, she touched her belt where the remote should be. The device was gone. "Oh, no," she moaned. "Is Jenna okay?"

"She's fine," Rourk assured her. "Where do you think you lost the remote?"

Aly had a flash, and ran out. A few seconds later, she came back in, the device clamped between her thumb and forefinger. It was dripping. "Must have fallen into the tub," she said through a weary groan. Hurrying forward, she scanned her child. "I was running water, so it was noisy in there. Did she fall again?"

"No. Can't you tell?" Attempting to remove a diaper tab, he remarked, "Little girls ought not to smell this bad."

When he glanced back at Aly, she was close enough to detect what he was talking about. Trying to keep a straight face, she said, "I'll try to get a law passed through Congress. What brought you in here, anyway?"

"I was going through some papers of Mother's. She had a habit of mixing valuable stock certificates with sentimental junk. But your daughter," he shook his head, "made it—difficult to work."

Aly pulled her lips together to keep from laughing. "I can't imagine how," she finally managed. "Would you like me to take over?"

Handing her the clean diaper he'd scrounged from the diaper bag, he stepped aside. "I presume Maude and Merle are once again engrossed in the Lusty Lunstroms?"

Aly deftly went to work, murmuring, "It's a lunchtime ritual."

"How do babies know exactly the wrong moment to do—that?" he muttered.

Aly fastened the diaper tabs and smiled. "You've just hit on the age-old question. Mothers and fathers for centuries have wondered the same thing." She lifted her daughter and, realizing she didn't have enough hands, said, "Here, hold her a second."

Pressing the child into his arms, she rolled up the disposable and walked to a far corner to a cardboard box labeled Trash and threw it inside. When she returned to the desk, she noticed that Rourk was wearing wire-rimmed glasses. Jenna had also noticed, for she was grabbing for them.

"I didn't know you needed glasses," Aly remarked.

"I don't to drink," he commented dryly, watching the child. "Only when I read."

"Oh, right. You were sorting through stock certificates and junk." Aly glanced down and saw a diploma, decorated with a red ribbon and embossed in gold, which read, "Valedictorian Collegiate Honors Academy, Rourk Andrew Rountree." She picked it up. There was the distinct imprint of a wet diaper in the document's center. "Oh, I'm so sorry," she murmured, surprised that this man had been the number-one student in a fancy prep school. "This is some of the 'junk'?" she asked.

"It has no value to me," he muttered as Jenna pulled his glasses down his nose.

"It looks important," she said, placing it where she'd found it. Her glance caught on a full tumbler of bourbon and a cigarette turning to embers in a marble ashtray on the far end of the desktop. Neither the glass nor the cigarette looked as though they'd been touched. Absently, she thumbed through several more papers. One from Stanford University snagged her eye. From what she could gather, Rourk had graduated summa cum laude. She squinted, confused. Stanford definitely wasn't an indulgent school that catered to lazy rich kids.

Swiveling to face him, Aly was struck with the incongruous beauty of the picture he presented. His glasses had been pulled askew across the bridge of his nose—a strikingly aristocratic nose, she noted. Jenna was alternately grabbing and releasing one wire temple piece, pulling the glasses lower with each tug.

"Oh, Rourk," she lamented, taking her daughter from him. "Why didn't you tell her no?" Jenna kept a stranglehold on the glasses, pulling them completely off Rourk's face. Aly had to pry her daughter's fingers loose to get them away from her.

When Aly handed them back, her fingers touched his, and she was jolted by the significance of the contact. Glancing up, she saw that he was quietly considering her. With a stab of conscience, she was reminded again that she ought to thank him for his good deed yesterday.

Rourk was a weak man, she knew. But she also knew there were degrees of weakness. Her father had never been as emotionally strong as her mother, but he'd managed to function, raise a family and keep a business afloat. It appeared Rourk might be an emotional level or two above her worthless ex-husband. But Aly had been through too much to allow herself to soften for *any* degree of weakness. She couldn't allow herself to be weak, and she wouldn't allow herself to fall for another weak man. Unfortunately, no matter what she wouldn't allow, she found herself harboring a soft spot for Rourk.

Hiking her baby up on one hip, she began, "Rourk."

After a pause that had grown overlong, he inclined his head and inquired, "What is it?"

"I—I just wanted you to know I—" She faltered and flushed. Mentally she screamed at herself, *What's the matter with you, dunderhead? Spit it out!* Spurred on by her scolding, she blurted, "Thank you for cleaning off the—er-wall, yesterday. It wasn't necessary, but I appreciate it."

A faint smile curved his lips. Those lips—so sexy and pouty when clamped around a cigarette—were twice as inviting when cast in a pleasant smile, and she felt an unanticipated flutter in her breast.

"You're welcome," he said. His eyes were pure, deep blue, and hypnotic. "You're very—very welcome...." His voice had fallen to a sexy husk that she could barely hear, which was odd, for his lips seemed suddenly quite close to hers.

But the proximity of his mouth wasn't nearly as shocking to Aly as the fact that her lips, on their own, had slanted upward and were poised as though inviting a kiss. She supposed it shouldn't have been any shock to her that he accepted that invitation, but when their lips met, a detonation of pure pleasure exploded in her brain. It was so unexpected, so volatile, she stopped breathing.

His mouth was warm, firm, but pliant against hers; seducing, yet gentle. His kiss was light, charmingly tentative, like the caress of a morning sun or the innocent brush of a baby's cheek. It soothed, but it also teased. He hadn't touched her anywhere but on her mouth. Still, she felt naked before him, and tingled with a demented urge to make bold love with him right there on the desk.

The magic of his lips against hers was so strong, so potent, yet in such a subtle way, she grew frightened by her eager compliance. Rourk Rountree was either the most sensitive of lovers, or the most shrewd seducer on earth.

If he'd simply grabbed her, she would have instinctively struggled and yanked free. If he'd thrust a probing tongue, she would have been incensed by his uninvited lust and slapped his face. But here he was, tasting her with the finesse of a connoisseur, savoring their kiss, this fleeting morsel, as though it were a feast. In his skillful way, Rourk was teaching her that even a brief physical communion could be vastly gratifying. Aly quivered with awe at this totally new experience.

Her brain jeered wickedly, *If he can create such havoc with barely a touch, think what delights knowing him fully could bring....*

Rourk very slowly, very deliberately pulled away. It was as though he knew, as though he read her mind, and with fiendish calculation withdrew from her on the brink of her surrender. Why? Did he expect her to beg?

She didn't dare, but she wanted nothing more in the world than the feel of his hands caressing her bare skin.

Her shiver of desire became a quake of regret. Too late, Aly realized he'd witnessed the disappointment in her eyes and she swung her gaze away. "You shouldn't have done that," she croaked, drawing in a long-overdue breath.

"I wanted to do it," he told her, his voice colored by hunger and something darker, possibly annoyance. She wondered with whom he might be annoyed. Perhaps with himself—for beginning something that had become more than he'd expected, more than he'd wanted? She hoped so, and she also hoped he'd keep his distance from now on.

Unable to help herself, she scanned his face. He wasn't smiling, and she could detect no inkling of his thoughts.

"You see, Mrs. Bean Fields," he reminded her, "shiftless bums do whatever they damn well please." He considered her for a moment, then murmured, "And, sweetheart—I was damn well pleased."

She could only stare as the compliment—if that's what it was supposed to be—took its time to sink in.

"Did you know I was married once?" he asked, startling Aly.

Still stuporous, she could just manage to get her head to move from side to side in response.

His smile grew thin. "I failed miserably at it, so don't get attached to me."

She blinked, feeling like she'd been slapped. His insolent warning had fallen completely out of the blue. "Why—I—" she stuttered, growing upset and angry. Had he gotten some crazy idea from their kiss that she was attracted to him? "I thought it would be plain for even a chunk of granite to see that I *loathe* you, Mr. Rountree," she hissed, resolved that her defiant remark was the absolute truth. "Don't worry your boozy head about my getting 'attached' to you. It could never happen!"

The grin he flashed was full-blown and devilish, so hot it curled her toes. "That's my girl," he drawled. Dipping his thumbs into his hip pockets, he strolled toward the door. "But, if you don't mind a suggestion," he called over his shoulder, "I'd say your loathing of my kisses needs work."

Aly gaped after him, dumbstruck. Heaven only knew how long she stood there contemplating the rapture of wringing his egotistical neck. How dare he suggest she enjoyed his kisses! She didn't. She loathed them—*it!* One infernal kiss! And she wouldn't let her mind dwell on it ever, not once. She swallowed. Well… Not often, anyway. And if she did chance to recall it, she would think of it *only*—Aly promised herself angrily—*only* with absolute disgust!

Jenna drew Aly back to reality, yanking on her mother's hair and prattling, "Dadadadadadadadada."

Aly glowered at her daughter's sweet face. Hefting the child higher on her hip, she trudged on leaden feet toward the kitchen, vowing, "Not if he was the last, spineless, conceited sleaze on earth, young lady. And don't you forget it."

LATE THE NEXT AFTERNOON, Rourk was heading in from a swim when he heard Aly on the kitchen phone. He paused in the act of drying his hair and listened. The conversation sounded interesting—something about condoms.

"Yes, Steve," she said. "I know how you feel about them, that's why I called you. You know you're always first on my list."

There was a pause, and Rourk stepped around the corner to better check out this risqué conversation. The young Mrs. Fields was perched on the corner of the kitchen counter, swinging a leg. He'd never seen her do that before.

So she was a leg swinger. Had she been lighthearted long ago? And at freak moments, when she didn't think she was being observed, did she revert back to it?

Rourk felt a brief stab of envy for this Steve person—a man for whom Aly would swing a carefree leg, and discuss condoms as though they were nothing more exotic than baseball bats.

She was wearing snug cutoffs that came halfway down her thighs. He took his sweet time observing her slender limb swing back and forth, noting its pale strength, contemplating the delectability of the feel of it locked in passion about his waist—

She laughed, dragging him back to reality. "I'll see you, then," she promised softly. "Meanwhile I'll send you a fax. I've got the number. Sure. I'll look forward to it. Goodbye." She hung up and hopped down. Whirling toward the door, she stumbled to a halt to see Rourk standing there clad in his wet swimsuit. By her expression it was clear she wasn't happy to witness such an expanse of bare male skin.

He looped the towel over his shoulders and grinned down at her, feeling oddly satisfied by her wide-eyed perusal. "Hi, Aly. Did I intrude on a private conversation?" She'd pinkened noticeably, and Rourk found that attractive.

"No. Auction business," she retorted, adjusting her shoulders and her expression to that I-don't-trust-you-so-don't-come-near-me scowl.

"Business?" he persisted, lifting a dubious brow. "Is it a business practice of yours to send obscene faxes?"

She was edging around the table, and he could see she was trying to decide how to manage her escape. When she began to hover near the pantry door, he decided she'd probably dash through to the dining room and, from there, to freedom. He pursed his lips, irritated. "I'm not going to attack you, Aly," he said abruptly.

She didn't visibly ease her stance. Apparently she not only thought he was a drunk and a womanizer, but a pathological liar into the bargain. "What was all that about condoms?" he asked finally, not sure why he gave a damn.

She swallowed, but to her credit, when she spoke, her voice sounded steady. "Aunt Merle found a huge hoard of antique condom tins in the attic this morning. I know several people who collect them, and was making calls to let them know about the rarer finds." Granting him her darkest scowl, she sniffed. "Obscene faxes, indeed. What a dirty mind you have, Mr. Rountree!"

She was so appealing at that moment, he had an urge to kiss her right then and there, but resisted. Instead he said, "And you have a dirty face."

She took a surreptitious swipe at her cheek, muttering, "The attic's a little dusty."

"And the pyramids are a little old," he quipped, enjoying her company. Aly Bean Fields had a pleasing effect on him that was more satisfying than a swig of booze. He took a step into the kitchen. The wood floor was warm against his bare feet. As he moved forward, he noticed that she took a step backward and a wry smile twitched at the corners of his mouth. She couldn't make a man more interested in pursuit by her charming retreat if she'd been trying, which he was sure she wasn't. "A huge hoard of antique condom tins?" he repeated, noting her renewed blush. What a beauty she was! And so full of sexual need. He didn't have any set plans to take advantage of *that*, but she was tempting—and he was weak, he reminded himself. Maybe too damned weak to resist her.

Aly nodded. "We figure about six hundred tins in all."

"Only six hundred?"

She shrugged, looking uncomfortable. "Maybe— er—six-fifty."

"That's more like it," he offered with mock seriousness. "It seems I'm not the first Rountree to be concerned about safe sex."

Her lips opened in stupefaction. "I— You don't mean to stand there and tell me you think any one man in your family could have been such a voracious Don Juan to use that many condoms. Why that's ridiculous. Someone was clearly a collector."

He flashed her a baiting grin, watching her wide brown eyes as she received his message—that she was a complete innocent when it came to Rountree-voracious Don Juanism. In all honesty, he was being terrible; he was being as base as Aly thought him to be. He had no idea where the condoms had come from, but he did know he loved getting a rise out of this tightly-wound, self-controlled woman.

He had a foolish desire to draw her out, see her laugh; and that went against his current plan to ignore and scorn the world in general. So he fought it. But an idea nagged. If he got her furious enough, maybe she'd strike out at him, and the fear damming up her emotions would burst, and she'd begin to heal from the hurt her ex-jackass had caused her.

That could be the stupidest idea he'd ever had. He didn't know. Being an aeronautical engineer didn't give him a license to practice psychiatry. Damn it to hell, he didn't even know why he was worrying about her. He had his own problems. Like, who the hell—and what the hell—he was?

But there she stood, little uptight Mrs. Bean Fields, plastered to the wall like a cornered rabbit, all eyes and hair. But with the bravest stiff upper lip he'd ever had the urge to pull into his mouth. She was afraid of him, but no more than he was of her. She represented something much more dangerous than a possible sex partner. There was something about her that cried out "commitment" and he didn't plan to set himself up for another failure of that magnitude.

He wanted badly, with every waking moment, to haul her to him, to make love to her. Half the time he tried to convince himself it would help them both in some way. But the other half of the time he knew it would probably hurt her more than it would help. He had nothing to offer her—nothing she wanted. She'd made that clear enough.

But sexually, she'd made something very clear, too. They were highly—explosively—compatible. The kiss told them things they'd have been better off never knowing. It had been a brash mistake. Rourk had known at once, and he'd been angry with himself the moment it was over.

The brief brush of their lips had told him how highly sexual she was, even standing there a foot away from him, clutching her baby, she'd been affected. Something powerful and unforgettable had passed between them and Aly had touched him in a way he'd never been touched by a woman. It excited him and nettled him and worried him.

He kept reminding himself he had nothing to give a woman—especially a woman with a baby and two shouting idiot savants. He didn't know if he could handle the responsibility. Didn't know if he wanted to. But Aly was a beauty, and she was so needy, and they were both in such pain—

"I—I'd better go," she sputtered.

Taking pity, Rourk stepped aside. "I said I wouldn't attack you, Aly," he reminded, his tone rueful. "Would you prefer I write it in blood?"

"Just leave me alone," she whispered brusquely.

AT SIX O'CLOCK, Aly's back ached as she stood beside the big kitchen sink wiping dusty condom tins with a damp sponge. Jenna was sitting in her high chair making crumbs out of a teething cracker, but gurgling happily.

Maude and Merle were clanking around the kitchen boxing up the last of a seemingly endless procession of freshly washed stoneware.

Dinner would be leftover spaghetti. Aly wasn't hungry. Her stomach churned with a persistent vision of Rourk, the great and lusty pioneer of safe sex. The picture was more stimulating than she cared to envision, but each time she grabbed the next condom tin, she saw the same erotic image. She'd erase it by rubbing each poor tin savagely, but invariably the next container would bring the specter back to her mind's eye: Rourk, clad in nothing more substantial than his tan, preparing to make love, albeit safely, the flash of his knowing, sexy smile as bright as a blinding camera flash in her brain.

She rinsed her sponge, squirting on additional kitchen cleaner and began to scour an embossed, hand-painted condom tin, grinding out a curse as she rubbed.

"What did you say, Aly?" Merle asked. "Something about ham? I don't think so. Spaghetti's all we have."

Aly jumped, unaware that her aunt had moved up so close behind her that she could detect her muttered profanity. "Uh— I didn't ask about ham. It was noth-ing important." Unhappy with her state of mind, she fibbed, "I was just wondering aloud how many of these things I have left to clean."

Merle eyed the pile of dusty condom tins and shook her head. "I would never have expected to find a col-lection of those things in this swanky mansion."

Aly had half a mind to tell Merle that Rourk had suggested these were not so much a collection as an ac-cumulation, but she decided against it. The subject had been preying on her mind long enough. No point in making it a topic of conversation.

"I sometimes wonder about the men in families that have boxes of these things in the attic!" Merle shouted.

Aly dropped the tin she'd just picked up and it hit the floor with a tinny clankity-clank.

"What do you mean, Merle?" called Maude as she pulled the bowl of spaghetti out of the microwave.

"I mean, how many of these were bought for—" She cleared her throat suggestively. "You know. Recrea-tional shenanigans around the house?"

"Really, Aunt Merle," Aly cut in, feeling flushed. "What difference does it make?"

"I mean, the family used the silver and the glasses and the furniture. Don't you think they probably used the—" she nodded meaningfully toward the sink "—the you-know-whats, too?"

Maude laughed and put the steaming leftovers on the long kitchen table. "Do you think anybody ever did you-know-what in here? On the dining table?"

Aly fumbled with another tin, but managed to catch it. Why did her mother and her aunt have to sound so much louder when they talked about sex? She wondered if Rourk was anywhere within shouting distance. She prayed he wasn't.

"Or had sex in the halls!" screeched Merle, now giggling with delight.

"Possibly," came an amused masculine voice. "And I'd wager the desk in the second-floor library has had many uses in its day."

Aly didn't dare turn around. However, she did turn a lively shade of maroon. Her body was frozen with mortification, her hands gripped around a helpless condom tin. She knew what he was talking about. It was horribly clear that he'd had the same thought as she when they'd kissed: to fall in a tangled heap on that desk and turn the good old summa-cum-laude sheepskin into something it had never been meant to be—a mattress. She sensed Rourk's scrutiny and her nape tingled. What was worse, she could even detect the teasing laughter in his gaze.

"Oh," Maude said, sounding a little embarrassed. "Hello, Mr. Rountree. I guess you heard what we were talking about."

"As did the people in Missouri," Aly mumbled under her breath.

"I caught a few vague remarks," he admitted overloudly.

Aly heard footsteps—not footsteps that tappy-tapped across a room the way chubby women in their late fifties might, but the solid thumping sounds of a man approaching someone he intended to harass.

"Need any help, Aly?" Rourk whispered very close to her ear.

She shook her head, refusing to look at him. "Why don't you sit down? Dinner's ready," she managed, tightly.

"What's this?" he queried, picking up a tin shaped like a wiener.

"It's a condom tin, Mr. Rountree," chirped Merle. "We found hundreds in the attic."

Aly fumed wordlessly. He knew exactly what they were and exactly where they were found.

"Very subtle," he shouted so the older women could hear.

"Vastly more subtle than you are!" Aly hissed.

Without comment, he set the tin wiener down.

Longing to upset him as much as he'd upset her, Aly dug around among the clean tins and slapped one into his hand. "Here, this is more your style," she snapped.

Out of the corner of her eye, she watched him turn it in his fingers, examining it. The tin was shaped like a big, open mouth.

"You ready to eat, Mr. Rountree?" Maude yelled.

Rourk chuckled, and held the tin toward Aly, whispering, "Well, well, sweetheart. I'll keep your offer in mind."

Pivoting away, he said more loudly. "Thank you, Maude. Suddenly, I'm very hungry."

Aly stared at the open mouth that lay in her hand and contemplated Rourk's husky remark. Why had it sounded so lecherous? What had he—

"Oh—my—*Lord!*" Aly cried, dropping the tin into the sink as realization hit. She'd handed Rourk the tin trying to tell him he was a big-mouth, and he'd managed to turn her insult into a sexual overture! Her skin burned with renewed mortification.

"What's wrong, Aly?" Maude asked in the middle of serving spaghetti to her sister. "I hope you didn't cut yourself. You'll need a tetanus shot."

Peering narrowly over her shoulder, she snagged Rourk's eye and ground out, "I don't need a shot for what ails me—I need a gun...."

Merle and Maude looked at each other, perplexed.

Rourk lounged in his chair regarding her with an academy award-winning expression of mild curiosity, as though he had no idea what could possibly be ailing her.

6

THE WIND WAS HIGH tonight, howling through crannies and gaps like a fretful banshee. Clawlike branches of a maple outside Aly's window clattered on the panes; and when a gust nudged the limbs just right, they made a sound against the rain gutter like fingernails scraping blackboard. Aly rolled over, muttering, "I'd get more rest stretched out on a highway at rush hour." Cars zooming past her head would be less unsettling than Rourk Rountree's shadowy, moaning mansion on this restless August night.

Throwing off the sheet that covered her, she padded over to the crib and checked on her daughter. Jenna was sleeping like . . .

Aly smiled to herself, understanding now where the phrase, "Sleeping like a baby," came from. Jenna looked precious lying there—a work of heavenly art, sprawled on her stomach without a care in the world. Apparently her child was going to be a heavy sleeper. Considering she'd napped all her life amid shouting people, her ability to sleep through anything shouldn't be difficult to understand.

But Aly wasn't a heavy sleeper, and tonight, with the mournful wind, she wasn't a sleeper at all. Quietly donning her cutoffs and an oversize T-shirt, she slipped into a pair of loafers and soundlessly left the room. She would use this time to number Mrs. Rountree's collection of R. S. Prussia plates. Tomorrow, she'd be taking pictures of several of them to include in the brochures, so the ninety-three plates had been stored in a room on the first floor they'd set aside for photographing.

As Aly headed for the stairs, she made herself face a certain bothersome truth. It wasn't just the wind that had kept her awake. It was Rourk. His sexy grin haunted her thoughts. His robust, bronzed body, glistening with droplets of water the way it had been after his swim, quickened her breathing against her will. His veiled, sexual innuendoes insinuated themselves into her brain, conjuring up heated fantasies of them tangled in each other's arms. These images crowded in to torment her each night after darkness fell, and she tossed and turned with her dangerous thoughts.

Tonight, her mental gymnastics had gotten the better of her. Though she'd tried everything she knew to put the shiftless devil from her brain, there'd been no way she could shake off her mind's erotic wanderings. And now, at two in the morning, here she was, bent on getting an hour or so of busywork done, simply to occupy an overstimulated mind that had trailed down a licentious path better left untraveled. Rourk was toxic to her mental health. It was just too bad she couldn't convince her raging female hormones of that.

Aly was far from perfect, herself. And this past week and a half around Rourk had brought back very vividly how really weak she was. So she worked that much harder at maintaining tight control over her emotions in order to deal with her fatal attraction to unreliable men. She didn't *want* to be attracted to Rourk, and she would get her mind off him if it took knocking herself unconscious with a tire tool.

She trudged down the stairs to the second floor and made quick work of scurrying to the main, curved staircase. She'd be double darned if she'd allow herself to lose any more sleep over him—after this next hour or so, of course. She was too worked up to go back to bed, yet. Besides, she'd meant to get those plates numbered today, anyway. It was probably a good thing— this windy night.

Her rationalizations all in place, she was bounding around the corner down the corridor toward the room with the plate collection when she was met by a broad-shouldered apparition. Aly gasped, startled to be confronted by the very devil she'd been trying to banish from her brain. By an unhappy coincidence, he was clad very much like she'd seen him in her unbidden fantasies: in a towel and nothing more.

He halted, too, and for a split second they stared at each other in mute surprise.

Rourk recovered first, slanting her a speculative gaze. "Hi, there," he drawled with a grin that made Aly's world teeter on its axis. "To what do I owe this unexpected visit?"

She drank in the sensuality of his supple physique. When she realized she was gaping, she tried to mask her sensual hunger, and worked at appearing unaffected. It was difficult.

His towel—unfortunately for Aly's peace of mind— was riding precariously low on his hips, revealing a tantalizing trail of dark hair that led from his navel on down to be greedily obscured by plush white terry cloth.

He flaunted a washboard stomach, tanned and taut, and a beautifully contoured chest, barely out of reach and simply begging to be caressed. Two steps—that's all it would take to touch him. Two steps. She clenched

her hands at her sides, not daring to trust her fingers
with their freedom, and stood stock-still.

Rourk was the picture of near-naked ease, while she
stood unnaturally stiff.

Aly was sure he'd seen the raw craving in her eyes
before she'd masked her reaction. She prayed she hadn't
been obvious, but she knew Rourk was terribly perceptive. She wouldn't put it past him to guess her hot-
blooded state of mind. Nevertheless, she had no choice
but to brave it out. "I—I was just going to do a little
work." With a sickly smile, she lied, "The wind . . . I
couldn't sleep."

He nodded, but said nothing. She recognized the fact
that his silence was a form of manipulation to make her
explain further, and she hated him for doing it. But the
silence and her own need to convince him that she was
not down there stalking him, forced her to babble on.
"I—I'd meant to number the Cavorting Cupid plates,
anyway. For the brochure, you know. We number everything and give a brief description in the brochure.
Like— Let's say, number twenty-seven might be Hearts-
and-Flowers Cupids, Blue And Silver. Like that. Takes
time, so it's just as well I couldn't sleep." Awkward
pause. "The wind and all . . ."

He nodded again. "You told me about the wind and
all," he reminded her, being singularly unhelpful.

"Oh, yes. Well, I'm taking pictures for the brochures
tomorrow. Did I say that? Anyway, this'll give me a
head stud." She bit her tongue in mortification. "Er—
start! Hot start!" She swallowed, mortified. Then, in
desperation, she enunciated crisply, "*Head start!*"

A flash of amused lightning fired his gaze. "Little
Aly—the sweetheart of Sigmund Freud," he drawled.

Aly winced, blurting, "For your information, not every slip of the tongue is Freudian!"

He took a step toward her, undaunted. "Then you don't think of me as a stud?" The query came out in a baiting whisper.

She retreated a step, but the wall halted further withdrawal. "No," she breathed. "I think of you as a bum. Besides," she frantically moved to the offensive. "What's your excuse for running around here almost naked?"

He pursed his lips as if giving the accusation due consideration. "I suppose—first, it's my house. Second, it's very late. Third, I was under the impression I was two floors away from prying eyes." Lifting an arm, he showed her a bottle of shampoo. "Fourth, I was out of this. Does that answer your question?"

She colored, humiliated. *One reason would have done.* "I see," she muttered, struggling for poise. "But if it's your intention to suggest I was down here to—to find you, you're sadly mistaken. I told you. I couldn't sleep."

He took another step toward her. "I know. The wind." His eyes held hers in a hypnotic vise, full of soft peril. "I couldn't sleep, either, Aly. But my problem had nothing to do with the wind."

Before she knew it, he was standing inches from her, his scent filling her head like an opiate. With either hand braced on the wall near her shoulders, he added, "I thought a cold shower might get my mind off a certain whiskey-haired woman. But since she's decided to seek me out, maybe she'd like to join me." The intensity of his burning blue gaze engulfed her. "What do you think?" he queried, his tone a velvety dare.

His expression was suddenly no longer teasing. He was serious. Deadly, disastrously serious. Deep-set eyes peered down at her, hooded and hot. Their sparking message was explicit. He was promising sexual fulfillment, assuring heady, climactic orgasms most women only dreamed of.

He inspected her closely, and Aly was sure he noted each fearful emotion that flitted across her features. He didn't touch her, didn't lower his face to hers. He simply observed her battle from the sidelines, a very unprincipled spectator.

He possessed great sexual power. Aly could sense it in some elemental part of her, and she trembled with that knowledge. Yet, deep within those expressive cobalt eyes, Rourk was also warning her that he had nothing else to offer her. Nothing she really needed—not commitment, not stability—just one volatile, exhilarating ride.

Tears of apprehension blurred her vision. Her beleaguered mind struggled valiantly with her traitorous body. Her mind was losing—or was she losing her mind? If she hadn't been so upset, she might have given in to wild, hysterical laughter. She must be losing her mind, or at least her hard-won good sense. She knew what she should do—*must do*—but she sizzled with wanting him, and her legs wouldn't heed her order to run. The two urgent needs that battled within her were irreparably separate, tearing at her soul.

"Well?" he coaxed, the single, mocking word hanging in the waiting silence of the deserted hallway. Sin gleamed in his eyes—charming, tempting sin—and Aly could feel her resolve draining away. Maybe he wasn't so bad, she told herself, recalling how nice he'd been to help with Jenna and that awful spider. Maybe—she toyed with her lower lip—maybe, this time, it would be different. . . .

"Good night, Aly," he said softly, grazing her cheek with a kiss. Unexpectedly releasing her from his encompassing arms, he inclined his head in a mute farewell. But before he turned to go, he tossed the shampoo bottle deftly from one hand to the other, his eyes never leaving hers. "Let me know when you're ready for—it," he offered with a rueful smile. "I'd be happy to share what I've got."

The remark had sounded strangely intimate, as though he'd been referring to some "it" decidedly more carnal than shampoo. She couldn't find her voice, but something fundamental inside her refused to accept his withdrawal, demanding that she do anything in her power to make him stay. Without reasoning why, or even daring to think about her actions, she reached toward him. Before she knew what she'd done, his towel was dangling in her trembling fingers.

He stilled, and half turned, his expression speculative.

"I—I—" she stammered, with no idea what to say in her defense.

He turned full on her, and she could see the results of her rashness. Apparently having a towel tugged off by a woman was a huge turn-on for a man, for Rourk was definitely that—definitely both—her mind boldly noted. "I don't know what came over me, Rourk," she whispered brokenly, appalled at herself.

His slow grin was without the slightest show of self-consciousness or repentance. "Evidently I don't make you as sick as I once did," he chided huskily.

She sucked in a breath. "Why— Why, you *planned* this!" she cried, not really believing it herself. Not entirely. But once she was within reach, he certainly hadn't fought her off!

His deep chuckle reverberating in the hall, he lifted her in his arms. "I plan nothing, sweetheart," he countered, carrying her toward his room. "That's the beauty of being shiftless."

Her heart pounded mercilessly against her breast. What was she allowing him to do? How stupid could she be? Even as she waged an internal battle, Aly curled her arms about Rourk's neck, relishing the feel of his nakedness against her bare arms, the clenching of his powerful biceps about her torso and legs. She sighed, hearing the contentment there, and wondering at herself.

"Rourk," she whispered against his throat.

"Yes, baby," he replied, his lips grazing her temple.

"We shouldn't do it."

"Oh, I don't know." He kissed her temple. "I think we both need this."

She closed her eyes, nuzzling the solid warmth of him, delighting in the quickened pulse-beat in his throat. "You're so right. We're both adults." She ran her tongue along the hollow there, feeling all at once very feminine and seductive. "We don't have to answer to anybody," she murmured. "If we want to have sex, then whose business is it?"

"That's true," he whispered. "But I was referring to the cold shower we both need."

As he spoke, Aly was deposited on the cool tiles of a shower stall. An instant later, a freezing torrent hit her skin. She shrieked and grabbed for support, catching Rourk about the waist. "What—" she choked, reflexively, while wiping water from her face. "What do you think you're doing!" she gasped flipping a long, wet strand of hair out of her eyes.

He helped her gain her balance, then pressed her firmly from him. "I'm taking a cold shower, Aly. I told you I was about to. Remember?"

She squinted at him with one eye, clutching herself and shivering violently from the frigid water. "What— Why? I thought you wanted me!" It came out in a defensive wail. "Instead, you dump me in here and try to give me pneumonia!"

He lifted his hand as though he wanted to smooth a strand of hair from her cheek. She lurched from his reach, then dashed from the shower stall and grabbed the first towel she saw, tugging it around herself with quaking limbs. "Don't you touch me, Rourk Rountree," she commanded tremulously, feeling hurt and rejected and foolish. "Don't you come near me—ever again!"

She grabbed a second towel, patted her face dry, then bent over to wrap it about her dripping hair. "I've never been so humiliated in my life, damn you!" she spat, surprised at the vehemence of her anger. It was all too clear that she was so devastated by his rejection it was impossible to hide.

He said nothing. Aly heard no sound but the thunderous pounding of cold spray. "Rourk!" she cried, wondering at herself for not spinning on her drenched loafer and escaping. "Are you listening to me, Rourk?"

"I hear you," he said finally. "And since you're still here I gather you haven't had enough."

Before she could react, long fingers appeared from around the shower curtain and dragged her back inside, towels and all.

This time, Aly was met with pleasantly warm water, and an impressive naked man lathered with soap. "Do I have to turn the cold back on?" he demanded grimly.

She blustered, blowing water out of her mouth and nose. "Let go—of me—you brute!"

She flailed out at him, pounding ineffectually on a sudsy mat of chest hair. The towel on her head uncurled with the added weight of the shower water and fell to the tiles with a loud *splat*. The one she'd been clutching about her had long since dropped away. "Rourk," she cried, frustrated in more ways than she cared to dwell on. "What exactly is the point of drowning me?"

"*Hell*, woman, you're not wearing a bra," he growled, releasing her as though she were suddenly a live electrical cord.

She stumbled backward against the wall. "Don't blame me. I didn't expect to be competing in a wet-T-shirt contest," she retorted, huddling in a corner. "Besides, you're the one with the shower fetish!"

He swore, and Aly glared up at his stern countenance. His hair was plastered to his head, ebony locks curling along his wide forehead. His lashes were spangled with liquid, making them sparkle like jewels. Water ran in tantalizing rivulets along the creases in his cheeks and dripped seductively, like slow-moving honey, from the cleft in his chin.

Patches of lather clung to his wide shoulders, and water cascaded in a pulsating, mesmerizing rhythm against the thick, shiny mat of hair on his chest. Aly had to force herself to glower. He was such a picture of manly perfection, it was hard not to simply stare in awe.

His expression closed further, but in something other than anger. Averting his narrowed gaze, he expelled a long breath. "Okay, I admit it. I like you, Aly." His gaze stole back. "Get out of here before I do something I regret."

She was stunned. "Get out of . . ." The echoed words trailed away, and she grew irate. "Get out of here before you do something you *regret!*" Punching his chest with an accusing finger, she spat, "You mean to tell me there's nothing about this—this brutality you regret, so far? Good grief, what would it take to make you regret something?"

He grasped her wrist, effectively putting an end to her thumping punctuation of every word. "I would make love to you, Aly. That's what I would regret."

She stilled and sobered. "What?" she whispered, sure she'd misunderstood.

His lips twitched in a sorry grin. "I would regret making love to you. Even shiftless bums have standards."

She felt a shaft of dismay. "And I'm not up to them," she concluded thinly. "Well, that's just fine." Yanking away from his hold on her arm, she added with a bravado she didn't feel, "I'm supremely grateful I'm not your type!"

"Maybe I should have said principles," he amended softly.

"Maybe you should go to hell!" she stormed, spinning away from him.

"I've been to hell, Aly. That's what I mean."

His cryptic statement, spoken in a fierce whisper, halted her as surely and swiftly as any physical restraint he might have used. Not wanting to, but with a powerful need, she faced him again. "You've said that

before," she pointed out, still glowering. She had a
sudden, overwhelming need to find out what made this
man so self-destructive. "What hell have you been to,
Rourk?" she asked more quietly, ignoring the torrent
that was steaming up the stall, but not quite able to ignore his bold nakedness.

"It's a long story." He watched her speculatively,
adding, "We'll run out of hot water."

She met his gaze, unflinching, and straightened, fully
aware that her breasts were brazenly exposed through
the soaked fabric, her nipples erect and goading. She
saw the effect her move had in the quick lift of his brows
and his intense, almost pained perusal. Still, he made
no move toward her.

When their glances met again, she allowed him to see
the encouragement in her eyes. She couldn't quite explain her feelings, but if there was one thing she could
recognize, it was strength. And Rourk had shown a
great deal in the past several moments. He was as hot
for her as she was for him, but he'd resisted the temptation to grab her and have his way with her. Unfortunately for Aly, he was still resisting. His strength was
there—dormant, perhaps—but there. No matter what
he said or what he thought. She liked the glimpse she'd
seen, and she didn't intend to leave—not just yet.
Sensing his mettle, she no longer fought his allure, but
allowed herself to be carried away by it. With a determined lift of her chin, she told him, "Then we'd better
not waste any more time just standing here, had we?"

In one swift movement, she lifted her T-shirt over her
head and let it drop to the shower-stall floor. It pleased
her to hear his low groan. She took a step toward him,
and the warm water hit her full force across her breasts.
She stood there, so near him as his gaze moved from her

eyes to her shoulders to her breasts, then back up. The prolonged anticipation was almost unbearable. He didn't move, and her body ached for his touch. "Aly," he whispered at last, his voice raspy and harsh with need. "I don't want to use you."

She shook her head. "I wouldn't let you. Rourk," she added, "what hell made you the way you are?"

A flicker of sadness marred his face. "The worst kind of hell," he said, his tone bitter. "The kind where you neglect your wife and baby, and then one day you come home and find them gone—forever."

She absorbed the confession with a tremor of compassion, her eyes never leaving his. There had to be more to the story than that. "What happened?" she asked.

"I thought I had everything under control, but really, everything was controlling me," he said gruffly.

"So you quit controlling anything, including your destiny?"

He grinned crookedly at her. "On the contrary, sweetheart," he objected, heavy sarcasm in his tone. "Every time I decide *not* to make a decision, I'm shaping my destiny."

He glanced away, his features taking on a harsh, distracted look. Aly sensed he was reliving the unhappy past that had destroyed his self-confidence, and her heart went out to him. Now, more than being merely hot for his raging masculinity and for the release of uncomplicated sex, she wanted to give this damaged human being a moment of unselfish tenderness. Very gently drawing him to the present, she placed her forearms on his chest and whispered, "Well, Mr. Destiny. Would you care to soap my back?"

His gaze dropped to meet hers, and the smoldering passion she saw there stunned her. He lifted a big hand to caress her jaw. The touch of his fingers was almost unbearable in its gentleness. "Are you sure?"

She nodded, turning into his hand and kissing his palm. "Very..." she murmured against his skin.

Reaching back to the soapdish, she picked up the bar of bath soap and placed it in his hand. Smiling encouragingly, she turned away from him.

She could feel him gather her hair and lay it forward over her shoulder as he began to lather her back. At first it was merely lovely, like a queen being cleansed by her handmaidens. But his hands—his long-fingered, expressive hands—could never be mistaken for any kind of maiden's. They were strong, exuding gentle power. Very soon, he was massaging her upper spine and Aly sighed happily, lowering her head as his thumbs relaxed her neck and upper back.

His touch trailed away from her nape as he pulled her against him and moved around to lather her belly. She could feel how aroused he was, and smiled at the contact, though her cutoffs were still a very real barrier between them.

He placed the soap in the dish and began to massage her stomach and the tender skin beneath her breasts. She moaned and leaned heavily against his chest. Stealing a look over her shoulder, she was thrilled to see that he was watching her. Boldly handsome, he smiled warmly down at her, murmuring, "How do you feel?"

"Overdressed," she answered dreamily.

His lusty chuckle hummed through her body as he began to softly manipulate her breasts between his hands. "It just means more playtime, sweetheart," he promised, bending down to nibble an ear and tempt her to the edge of sanity with his tongue.

He turned her to face him and pulled her body, slick with suds, against his, kissing her hungrily, thoroughly. Against her mouth he urged, "Let's get rid of those shorts—now."

When she nodded and moved slightly away to reach down to unfasten the waistband, he swept her fingers away with, "I think I can make it more . . . interesting."

Lowering himself to his knees, he began to slowly, deliberately undo her shorts. With every released snap, he placed a hot kiss against her belly, moving lower, ever lower. Aly could do little but grasp his shoulders for support; her legs had become frightfully unsteady.

When the shorts fell in a soggy heap, Rourk took his time pleasuring her, his strong hands urging her pelvis into more intimate contact with his tender ministrations.

Aly closed her eyes and groaned, clasping his head to her. "Oh, Rourk," she whispered languidly, relishing the heightened sensations his lips and tongue were eliciting. "I knew . . ." She sighed. And very soon, her sigh became a whimper of pleasure. A cry of pure joy.

Too weak to stand, she sank to the shower-stall floor, which was now cushioned with towels and clothing. She'd never felt so free. This man, this master of pleasure, now knew her in a terribly intimate fashion. That thrilled her, made her want to pleasure him, to know the ultimate in ecstasy with him. Needing to feel him inside her, she pleaded, "Love me, Rourk."

He settled over her, and kissed her throat, nipping along her jaw toward lips throbbing with need. She loved the steamy dreamworld they were lying in, the warm stream of water that caressed and stimulated. She

loved the feel of his tongue on her lips, his teeth on her
cheek, but she craved, thirsted after—was dying for—
his thrusting, erotic essence, deep inside her. She
yearned for the carnal thrill of being one with him.

"Take me, Rourk," she cried in a thready whisper.
"Love me...."

He lifted his face from hers, his eyes hot with desire.
"Not yet, darling," he said. "You won't mind the wait,
I promise."

Before she could beg him to relent, he claimed her lips
with his—hard, hot and dominant. Her mind whirling
with urgency and confusion, she held him tightly
against her, pulling him close, scratching his back.
Lifting her legs, she stroked his hips with her thighs, and
ran her foot along the back of his hard haunch, moaning as his kiss sent a new spiral of delight through her.

But her mind echoed his hoarse vow, *Not yet, darling. You won't mind the wait, I promise.*

What did he mean? She didn't know or care. She was
only certain that she would find out, in Rourk's own
good time, and no power under heaven could drag her
away from him now—not until he finished what she'd
started....

7

WHEN ROURK LIFTED HIMSELF away from Aly to turn off the water, she lamented her displeasure and caught his hand. With a roguish laugh, he pulled her up to stand beside him.

The steamy shower stall was a paradise of slippery stimulation as they toweled each other dry, replacing the arousing friction of thick terry with the even more stimulating sensation of lips, tongue and teeth.

They had brought their bodies to a fever pitch of need when they emerged into the cool sting of the air-conditioned bathroom, and she shivered. Rourk was holding her hand, but he turned her into his arms to warm her, nuzzle her cheek, stroke her back and buttocks with knowing fingers.

The intimate proximity of their bodies told Aly that he was ready for lovemaking, and she rubbed against him, letting him know that she, too, was nearly bursting with desire.

With a low chuckle, he kissed her ear, whispering, "Would you rather make love on the desk upstairs, in the hall or on the grand piano?"

His tongue in her ear sent a quiver of delight through her body, and she curled her arms about him, sighing, "I think . . . the bed."

He shifted slightly away to look down at her. She smiled up at him, at his teasing expression. "The bed?"

he queried. "There are nearly twenty beds in this place. *Which* bed?"

She kissed his furry chest, murmuring, "I was hoping nearly twenty, but if you don't think you're up to it . . ." She allowed the taunt to trail away and gave him a challenging look through lowered lashes.

He growled and lifted her away from the ground so quickly she gasped. "I'll show you who's up for what," he vowed, laughing now.

He deftly skirted an old shipping chest at the foot of his rough-hewn bed. Thick planks fashioned into a headboard and footboard gave the huge bed a feeling of ruggedness, sturdiness—like the man who slept there.

His room was medieval in flavor, with a dropped-soffet ceiling, adoquin stone floor and copper fittings and fixtures.

She squealed as he dumped her into the middle of his large bed and she drew up on her knees, backing toward the headboard, delighting in the game of caveman conquering cavewoman. She hadn't played sex games with a man in so long. . . .

Her back to the rough headboard, she asked, "What are you going to do?"

He grinned and moved toward her, reaching out and grasping an ankle. His fingers went around it possessively, gently, yet with authority. "Apparently, I'm going to indulge someone in a game of catch-me."

She grinned back, reveling in the harsh texture of the wood against her back juxtaposed to the luxurious softness of his hunter-green velvet bedspread. She delighted in the fantasy of being a buccaneer's captive. "Let's pretend," she said, sounding breathless, "that you're a pirate and I'm someone you've captured, and you're going to have your way with me."

His grin twisted devilishly. "That sounds like rape, sweetheart. I don't think that's what you really want."

She eyed him with playful speculation. "Okay, then *I'll* have to have my way with *you*."

She moved to her knees and took hold of his shoulders, slipping her arms about him and drawing her breasts up to meet his lips. "You're my prisoner," she whispered sternly, laughter in her tone.

He groaned, hugging her to him.

"Lie down on your back," she commanded.

He kissed the rise of her breast, then nibbled.

She giggled. "Rourk, I'm having my way with you. Now you flip onto your back."

He ignored her command and continued pleasuring one taut nipple. She grew weak and sighed languorously. "You're a very bad prisoner for disobeying me. I may have to punish you."

"I may let you," he whispered roughly.

He tugged and she moaned, drawing him even closer. "Rourk . . ." she reprimanded thickly. "You're not playing the game."

"Oh, baby," he murmured against her breast. "I'm starting to get real . . . serious."

Aly loved the hoarse, almost-pained tone of his voice, his torrid breath on her cool skin.

Aware of her complete surrender, Rourk lowered her to the velvet as he continued to explore and excite with his teeth and mouth and hands.

She reached for him. Encircling his erection with her fingers, she evoked a shudder from him and his kiss deepened.

As her stroking increased, his tongue held her more and more spellbound with his expertise. It seemed the more she attempted to excite him, the more he elicited heightened desire in her.

At last, he lifted his face from hers, murmuring huskily, "Don't go away."

With that, he slid to the edge of the bed. Instead of obeying him, she pulled up on quaking elbows and cried weakly, "Don't leave me."

He chuckled and turned back to drag her to his side. "Sweetheart, I wouldn't leave you now if the place was burning down around our foolish heads."

Then she saw what he was doing. He was opening a condom packet. Instantly taking control, she swept his hand away. "Let me," she whispered.

As she sheathed him, he closed his eyes and lay back with a long, low sigh. This very intimate moment between them was exciting for Aly, and when she was finished, she slid up to straddle him, dropping wet kisses across his chest, nipping provocatively as she moved her attentions gradually forward. "This is what you wanted us to wait for?" she breathed. "This is why we couldn't make love in the shower?"

He looked at her and grinned as she slid up to dangle tempting breasts above his lips. "Yes," he admitted quietly. "This isn't a good decade to be careless. I may be weak, but I'm no fool."

She cast a sparkling glance over her shoulder toward the protracted evidence of his fervor, and whispered slyly, "At the moment—sweetheart—you don't *look* very weak."

Laughing gutturally, he grasped her by the waist and settled her atop him, declaring, "Compliments will get you the best I have to give."

The initial sensation of his erection made Aly groan with pleasure. With total abandon, she lowered herself to take him inside.

Rourk whispered a sweet blasphemy and began to move, causing her to cry out with surprise and gratification. He knew how to summon a surge of delight with each subtle motion.

She arched her back, bracing her arms on his shoulders as he thrust. Her body damp with exertion, she lay forward over him, her fingers entwined in his hair as they moved in unison. In her dizzying drive toward ecstasy, she whimpered near his ear, "Rourk . . . I'm going to—faint. . . ."

He kissed her earlobe, assuring lustily, "It's not fainting you're going to do, babe. . . ."

He plunged hard, again and again, and she cried out. Then her body burned with the sweet, molten sensations of total release.

At the same time she could feel his male orgasm pulsating within her. His arms wrapped around her and held her to him with an ardor that was both thrilling and startling. Her lips curving in pure happiness, she collapsed, sated, on his broad chest, thrilling to the heavy beat of his heart.

They lay, drained, for long minutes, until their dampened bodies started to chill. Rourk began to stroke her back, his long fingers massaging and warming. After a lovely moment, his hands were on her buttocks, and he was pressing her to him. At the same time he was lifting his hips to lock them deeply together. Aly sucked in a startled breath to discover that he was ready to make love again, but before she could form words, he nuzzled her throat and murmured, "I hate to do this, but I'm going to have to slip out of you, sweetheart."

She sighed a little sadly, and hugged him tightly. "Why?" she whispered.

"You're chilled." He patted her rounded hip. "Wouldn't you like to warm up under the covers?"

She clamped her thighs around him and did a pert thrust of her own. He moaned with surprise and pleasure. "That doesn't answer my question," he said hoarsely.

"Okay," she lamented at last, brushing his lips with hers as she said, "I'll let you go, but not for long."

He chuckled and with the flexing of a powerful thigh, turned her gently on her side, sliding from her warmth.

Aly closed her eyes at the sexy feel of their parting. She allowed him to tuck her gently beneath the covers, never opening her eyes, never wanting to. She preferred to remain cloistered in her sightless world of tactile gratification.

She heard him open another condom packet, and shivered with new anticipation. When he rejoined her beneath the covers, she took him into her arms and lifted her lips for a kiss. He didn't disappoint her, and the kiss they shared was the dizzying beginning of another flight into the impetuous realm of wild, scorching pleasures of the flesh.

ALY LAY ON HER STOMACH, her cheek against sheets redolent with the scent of their lovemaking. Her arousal was heightened by the feel of Rourk's hands as they insinuated their way beneath her body, each hand lovingly cupping a breast.

He was blanketing her, and they were blissfully joined. Aly felt drained but deliciously decadent as he whispered naughty things in her ear—naughty, sexy words that made her tremble and smile. But her throat was so blocked with emotion she couldn't speak.

He chuckled at her reaction, and the resonance of it tingled through her. She wanted to hold him badly, so she reached up and clutched his wrists. He moved within her and she sighed. He moved again and she moaned, crying out his name. He pressed more deeply and she experienced another unexpected orgasm. Grasping at him, and with a half cry, half sigh, she said, "No more—I don't have the strength...."

He kissed the curve of her ear. Then, sweeping away her hair, he kissed the nape of her neck, murmuring, "Your pleasure turns me on."

Exhausted laughter gurgled in her throat. "In that case, we may be here forever."

He nibbled along her shoulder. "Eternity would be a wonderful place—spent right here."

His knowing thrust gained her undivided attention and she moaned contentedly, stroking his wrist with her thumb. "Umm-hmm. But I think we need to get some sleep."

His hands kneaded gently. "Can't you sleep like this?"

"Oh, yes...." She sighed. "Just don't move."

His chuckle rippled through her again, and with a mocking sulk in his tone, he said, "Spoilsport."

She lay there contentedly for a blessed span of time, and was falling asleep when he lifted himself from between her thighs.

"Why are you deserting me?" she asked sleepily.

"I can't sleep this way," he groused gently. "It's too much of a temptation."

She shifted to her side to smile at him. "You're an animal." It was a soft, loving murmur.

Resettling himself beneath the covers, he gathered her to him. "You're not exactly a dishrag in bed, yourself," he whispered, his lips against her temple.

He drew her into the crook of his arm and stroked along her collarbone with a feather-light touch. "I thought I'd had great sex in my life . . ." he began, but didn't go on.

Aly snuggled close, knowing a flutter in her breast at his unfinished, but meaningful statement. Hugging him to her, she admitted rather ruefully, "I had years of great sex."

He stopped stroking and peered down at her. "Better than tonight?"

He sounded strangely hurt, as though it had never occurred to him that she might have had a hotter sex life with another man. She kissed his chest. "No, Rourk . . ." was all she could manage. She didn't have the words to tell him, but she'd never had mere hot sex affect her the way it had tonight. Wanting to make him understand, she said, "Sex was about all Jack did with any degree of enthusiasm. Except drink—"

She frowned, cutting herself off. Suddenly everything they were doing had the ring of déjà vu. What exactly was she doing here—in a shiftless do-nothing's arms having crazy-wonderful sex? *Repeating the same old mistake. That's what you're doing, idiot!* Her blood ran cold, and she found herself in need of space—distance. She had to think rationally, get away from Rourk's sweet, erotic demands and get her head on straight.

Pressing against him, she backed off, scrambling up to sit. "What have I done?" she mourned aloud. Though the room was dark, Aly's vision was accustomed to it and she could see Rourk's perplexed expression.

He reached for her, placing a hand on her knee. "You've done quite a lot in the past couple of hours. What exactly can't you recall?"

She hastened from his touch and slid off the other side of the bed. "I'm not kidding, Rourk. I've made a terrible mistake. I—I can't believe I'm doing the same stupid thing again!"

Scurrying to the bathroom to get her clothes, she came to an abrupt halt when she remembered they were lying in a soaked heap in the shower stall. Her gaze darted around the bathroom. No dry towels.

Whirling toward the bathroom door, she was struck dumb to see a very large, very irritated, naked man blocking her exit.

"What the hell, Aly," he demanded. "I thought we'd moved beyond that you-feckless/me-flawless attitude of yours. So you had sex with me. So what? You're still fairly competent. I bet the Auctioneer's Association of America might only ban you from the business for five, maybe ten years because of this."

He was glowering at her. She had an urge to take a step back, but knew in her heart he'd never hit her, though his face was etched with wrath. But his blue eyes registered more hurt than anger, and she felt a twinge of guilt over what she'd done. She—the woman always needing to be in control—had started this. *Her* weakness—*her* imperfection—had caused this; not his.

She averted her gaze. "I—I'm sorry, Rourk. I know I'm as much to blame here as you, but I can't help how I feel."

"And just exactly how is that, sweetheart?" he chided. "Let's get it said, now, while both of us are naked and angry. Let's get it said, so the next time you tug off my towel, I'll know it's simply because you're out of clean laundry."

She flinched, but managed to face him directly. She supposed he deserved something. After several false starts, when she opened her mouth and nothing came out, she cleared her throat and tried again, "Look, Rourk—I—I don't have anything against you, personally. Not really."

He eyed her with a skeptical lift of a brow, but said nothing. He only stood there, his legs braced apart, fists on hips, all taut-and-tensed male animal. She chewed on her lip and went on, "You're so—good-looking, and sexy, and I don't think you're exactly like Jack was, but you're not what I'm looking for in a man."

He nodded, pursing his lips as though absorbing that news. "Am I too large or too small?" he demanded.

Her cheeks flamed, her mind crying, *You're anything but too small!* But she forced herself to remain on the subject at hand—which was definitely not a complaint about his physical attributes.

She cleared her throat again. For some reason it had become painfully dry. "Don't joke. I'm serious. It's just that—that my dad was sort of . . . ineffectual. At least he tried, but he made bad decisions. Then came Jack." She ran her hands distractedly through her damp and tangled hair. "When we first met, I thought he was strong—everything my dad hadn't been. But as soon as life started treating him badly, he fell apart. And, as so often happens, a man with no control over his own life has to dominate those around him."

She paused to steady her breathing, which was coming in shallow, labored pants. "And, then there's you. Tonight I found myself in the middle of making the same mistake with you I made with Jack. You're both charming, sexy, shiftless quitters."

"Hell, don't bother to sugarcoat it, sweetheart," he ground out scornfully. "Give it to me straight."

She felt so guilty she could hardly face him, but she had to get this said once and for all. Her voice thin with anxiety, she pleaded, "Oh, Rourk. Don't you understand? I *can't* get involved with you. It's as simple as that. Surely—" Her voice broke and she shook her head. "Surely there's a great guy out there who's holding down a job, who won't hit me, who wants a normal, average life—who can also turn me on in bed." Tears blurred his image. "I... I plan to find him one day, and he won't be *you*. I guess, tonight, I had a need for some good old uncomplicated sex, and there you were—practically naked...."

"I was handy. You were horny. Check," he retorted with grim contempt.

She smothered a sob. It was horrible to stand there facing the man who had just given her so much selfless pleasure and tell him in so many words she thought he was little more than gutter trash.

Anguished, she muttered, "I can't help it if I don't respect you, Rourk. I just can't let myself fall in love with you." With a brave lift of her chin, she demanded, "Please get out of my way so I can leave. The sooner this episode is forgotten, the better!"

He did as she asked, but as she made her escape, he grasped her by the arm, spinning her to face him. Before she knew what was happening, he'd pulled her against him and was kissing her hard. He moved his lips harshly over hers, devouring their softness, as he held her in a savage vise. She fought against his anger, her fists clenched against his chest, but her body experienced a flash fire of renewed desire. Even in his fury, he was all-too-knowing in the ways of women.

With a suddenness that made Aly almost lose her balance, he released her, demanding harshly, "Forget *that*, sweetheart."

She could only stand and blink, her body humming with a mixture of hunger and rage as he strode to a set of double doors. Opening them, he rummaged briskly for a moment before he located what he was seeking.

Aly found a man's terry robe thrust at her with the sharp-edged comment, "Don't thank me. Our little heart-to-heart was thanks enough."

He stalked through the bathroom door and slammed it at his back. After a minute, Aly's numbness wore off enough for her limbs to respond to commands. Slipping into the huge robe, she lurched unsteadily from Rourk's room, working very hard at putting the "episode"—as she chose to call it—from her brain. But her unruly mind taunted back, *Use all the euphemisms you want, sweetheart. The memory isn't going to go away!*

ROURK SAT TILTED BACK in a chair in the kitchen, his loafered feet crossed at the ankles and resting on the kitchen table. He was scowling. He knew he was scowling because Maude and Merle kept peering covertly at him as they prepared breakfast. If he hadn't been in such a foul mood, he might have laughed out loud at their pixielike ruminating gazes.

Damn that Aly Bean Fields! She planned to forget their sultry tumble between the sheets, did she? Well, that was just fine and dandy with him. Shiftless bums got sex when and where they could find it, and last night had been a sexual windfall of the highest magnitude. But unfortunately, last night hadn't been just any night of casual sex, and no amount of fooling himself was going to change that.

Damn it to hell. He liked Aly. Respected her. Now there was irony for you. He respected her and she made no secret that she thought he was a worthless slug.

Another irony hit him in the gut. Since he'd met Aly, for the first time in a long time, he liked himself—for brief smatterings of time. Even felt moments of strength of character when he was with her or her baby daughter.

He'd always been strong—all his life—in order to get his father's attention. Maybe not strong—maybe *aggressive*. He'd aggressively sought his father's blessing. Then, when everything went to hell, he'd realized his mistake. He'd been living his life for his father—not for himself. He'd aggressively, blindly, become someone he didn't know or like.

And now that he was—in brief moments—actually liking himself because of Aly, Little Mrs. Bean Fields was telling him he was an "episode" she planned to forget. He laughed harshly. *What satire we make of our lives!*

Apparently his bitter chuckle was louder than he'd intended, for Merle peered over her shoulder from the stove where she was scrambling eggs.

"Want another cup of coffee, Rourk?" she shouted, looking worried.

He took his feet off the table and shook his head.

"Anything wrong?" Merle asked as she moved the heavy skillet to the counter and scraped the eggs onto a platter alongside a pile of bacon and sausage. "Didn't you sleep well?"

Sleep well? Hell! He snorted, deciding he'd better make an effort to be civil. A shouted third-degree, he didn't need. With a polite smile that made his face ache, he yelled, "Slept like a dead man."

Merle eyed him speculatively. It was obvious she thought he looked like one, too. "The wind keep you up?" she asked, not buying his lie. "Aly's sleeping in. Said the wind kept her up most of the night." She shook her head and appeared confused. "I can't understand it. I didn't hear a thing."

Rourk smiled, this time with genuine amusement. Evidently these women had no intention of admitting they were hard-of-hearing, not even if they failed to catch the sound of a jet plane crashing through the roof of the kitchen.

"Get the toast, Maudie," Merle screeched, changing the subject.

Just as the two portly women sat down, Aly appeared at the kitchen door, carrying her daughter. Since it was well after seven, the young Mrs. Fields had taken great liberties with her work schedule.

"Oh," yelled Maude. "Morning, daughter. Seems Rourk couldn't sleep last night, either."

Aly closed her eyes for the briefest second, but Rourk could tell she was flinching with the overloud reminder of the "episode." It was clear that she hadn't had much sleep after she'd left his room, and he felt somehow vindicated. He didn't want her to forget. He wanted her to be tormented by the recollection just as he was.

He gave her a casual nod and a twisted grin, but he knew the friendly expression didn't extend to his eyes. Therein was the real message, and it was an angry, frustrated one.

She nodded back, however stiffly, and settled Jenna in her high chair.

"It's about time, sleepyhead," Merle said, turning to see her niece for the first time. "You look horrible."

Aly cast Rourk an irascible look and went about fixing Jenna her cereal. "Thanks a bunch," she ground out, then covered a yawn.

"Must have been some wind," Merle put in loudly just as Aly slid into her seat beside Rourk. "I mean to keep you both up so late."

Aly didn't respond but proceeded to assist Jenna in grasping her baby spoon.

"Funny," Her aunt went on. "Maudie and I didn't hear a peep."

Rourk watched Aly surreptitiously as she served herself some eggs. Her expression was grim, her demeanor stiff.

"I heard something," Maude interjected. "About three o'clock I was at the foot of the main staircase on my way to the kitchen for a snack. I thought I heard a loud moan. Weirdest wind I ever heard." She grimaced in thought. "Sounded more like that scene in that movie—oh I can't remember the name—but those two hotbloods were making wild, loud love in the taxi."

Aly's fork, halfway to her lips, began to shake, raining eggs in her lap. She didn't seem to notice, for her eyes were closed.

"Really," Merle screeched, staring at Maude. "Ghosts, you think?"

"We don't have ghosts roaming our halls," Rourk supplied helpfully.

Aly cast him a dagger-filled glance as Maude shrugged and yelled back, "Well, of course not. Had to be the wind. But it was sure wild."

Rourk picked up his coffee mug and sipped. His sidelong look snagged Aly's and from behind his cup he whispered, "She's right. I remember that moan."

Aly colored fiercely and seemed to have trouble swallowing her food.

"Would you care for a cup of coffee, Mrs. Bean Fields?" he asked casually.

She didn't answer.

"Aly," Merle called loudly across the short distance. "Rourk asked you a question."

Aly finally managed to swallow. "I'll get my own coffee," she mumbled, and hopped up from the table.

He lifted his mug toward her. "I could use something hot," he said.

Glaring at him, she hissed, "I hope you'd like it in your lap!"

With a smile of mock civility he taunted under his breath, "Oh, baby... And I thought you didn't want me."

Going wide-eyed, Aly choked.

Rourk set his mug down and glowered at his plate. Not one of his more gallant moments. But damn the woman. When would she realize being perfect wasn't possible? And that making love with him hadn't been the end of the world. She'd make herself crazy with her I-have-to-be-better-than-anyone-in-the-world problem—and she'd hurt everybody she loved along the way.

He ought to know.

8

IT WAS NINE O'CLOCK in the evening, and Aly was beat. She'd just finished putting address labels on over four thousand brochures, and they were bundled up and ready to be mailed in the morning. The first auction was only a week away, and there was still too much to do.

She checked on Jenna and, thankfully, the little girl was asleep. Slipping the newly repaired monitoring remote on her belt, Aly headed toward the kitchen to see what might be left for dinner. It had been one rough week since she'd so foolishly allowed herself to have sex with Rourk. Every day, almost hourly, she found herself reliving one sultry moment or another between the sheets with him, and a shiver of dread would run through her.

This "episode" of theirs was going to be as hard to remove from her brain as a thirty-year-old price tag stuck on a piece of crystal.

Rourk had certainly been no help in the matter. It was evident that he planned to bait her with his provoking grin and glittering eyes until she screamed for mercy.

Once, a few days ago, when she hadn't known he was near, he'd whispered urgently in her ear, "Here comes your aunt. Quick, act like we never had sex!"

She'd jumped, spun and scattered a drawerful of bobby pins and curlers all over the floor. He ambled casually away while Aunt Merle looked distressed and shouted, "When I asked you to help me dump trash, I meant in the trash box, not all over creation!"

Aly glared at Rourk's receding back, but had been helpless to retaliate.

So she decided her best course was to avoid him. Blast his unrepentant hide! He'd walked into her life and with the speed and heat of a fire in dry grass she'd turned into a raging bundle of need. It felt too much like weakness. She didn't like the feeling, and intended to avoid its sexy, vengeful source at all costs.

High-pitched laughter met her as she entered the kitchen. Both Merle and Maude, washing dinner dishes, were watching the home-shopping channel. Aly felt a momentary tingle of apprehension, but before she could really become upset, she realized neither of them was actually phoning in.

"What's so funny?" she asked, loudly enough to be heard.

Maude turned from her drying. "Oh, hello, dear. There's a chicken-salad sandwich and some sliced tomatoes for you in the fridge."

As Aly settled down at the table, she glanced at the set. A beautiful pair of hands with ten perfect, bright red nails, was displaying three strands of faux pearls, explaining how nice they would be for birthdays, anniversaries, and so on. Aly turned away and tried again. "What was so funny when I came in, Mother?"

Maude put away the plate she was drying. "You'll never believe this, Aly. It seems this lady named Leona was calling from her house to order a pair of silver seahorse earrings, and she said she had to hurry 'cause the house was burning down!"

Aly halted with her sandwich halfway to her mouth. "Her what?"

Merle chimed in, "Leona said she loved the home-shopping channel and she bought the matching sea-horse necklace last month, and had to have the ear-rings. Apparently a grease fire in her kitchen had gotten out of control and she'd just put her two cats in the car to move them to safety, but had forgotten her car keys. When she ran back in the house, she saw the ear-rings come on the set and risked her life and called."

Maude, grinning ear to ear, nudged her sister indicating she wanted to take over. "Picture it! This woman's kitchen was blazing and carpet in the living room was starting to smolder while Leona chatted away. So Allison—" Maude pointed to the hands on the TV screen "—that's her—well, Allison said, 'We'll save you a set of earrings, Leona. Now get the hell out of your house!'"

"I don't believe this," Aly said. "When did that happen?"

"Five minutes ago. We heard it," shouted Merle.

Aly shook her head. "You're kidding. Nobody would do something that crazy."

"Swear!" Merle crossed her heart with a sudsy hand. "And you said *we* were addicted!"

Aly took a bite of her sandwich and swallowed before she responded. "Okay, you're not quite *that* addicted. But you still aren't buying anything, are you?"

"No," Merle said. "But it's painful. A little while ago, they showed this polyester horizontal-stripe toga in red and blue that would have been perfect for those fall evenings out on the porch."

Maude laughed, "Yeah, if you want to masquerade as a big, fat flag."

"At twenty-nine ninety? It would have been a bar-gain at twice the price."

"Never mind, you two," Aly put in, cutting up a slice of tomato. "Besides, Mother, our apartment doesn't have a porch."

"Oh," yelled Maude. "That reminds me. That black dress I ordered for you and that sequined sweatsuit were delivered to the apartment today when I dropped by to pick up the bills."

Aly squinted up at her mother, her expression wary.

"I sent them back," Maude said, making a rankled face. "But mark my words. One day, you'll wish you had that dress."

Aly ate a bite of tomato and shook her head. When she'd swallowed, she said, "Let's get some money in the bank before we worry about slinky black dresses for me."

Maude harrumphed. "I keep telling you, this Rountree job will give us a real nest egg. I've been doing some calculating, and I figure our commission on this, even with outlay for brochures, ads and extra help, we're finally out of the red for the first time in fifteen years! We'll meet our current needs for quite some time with our fifteen-percent commission, and even have some to put aside. And since you've incorporated us, we're in a lot better position, tax-wise." She gave her daughter a prideful smile. "We can afford a few new things since you're such a savvy businesswoman."

No one said anything for a minute. Aly knew they were all thinking about how tough life had been for years with Ben's well-meant, but lackluster business acumen.

It was true that Mrs. Rountree had thrown Ben the business because they'd been friends years ago in school. But it was also true that Aly had worked like a dog organizing, managing and orchestrating the job into a top-notch, well-oiled success-in-the-making. It was becoming more and more obvious that Aly, though nervous about taking the company reins, was making a real difference in their financial prospects.

While talking up this auction with contacts across the country, she'd managed to line up four more for the next couple of months. Though not of this magnitude, they were solid business deals that would add to Bean Auction's reputation and ultimately to its blossoming finances. Also, she'd gotten in touch with several well-respected "finders" who bought and sold at the most prestigious auctions, finding items for wealthy collectors. Their contacts would be invaluable in future business dealings.

Still uncomfortable about any added expenses, Aly decided to relent—slightly. She knew her mother didn't make mistakes where figures were concerned. "We'll see." She sighed. "Maybe we can manage a board meeting in a couple of weeks and decide on a few things."

Maude made a tsking sound. "You worry too much."

Aly shrugged. "I can't help it. I suppose it's—you know—our past." Seeing her mother's features sag, she said, "Okay, Mom, since your birthday's coming up in September, maybe we can manage to do something a little special."

Maude put her hands on her well-padded hips and grinned. "I have an idea. You can get me a home-shopping gift certificate. That would be item number fifty-five if anybody's taking notes," she added with an elfin twinkle in her eye. "Then on my birthday we can eat cake and watch the channel until I see something I want." Aly's apprehension must have been apparent, for her mother amended, "Under thirty dollars?"

With a resigned smile, Aly nodded. "Deal."

"Somebody playing poker in here?" a male voice inquired from the door, causing Aly to freeze in a sandwich-to-the-lips position.

"No, Rourk." Maude laughed wiping her hands dry. "We're having a high-level financial meeting with Simon LeGree, here."

"Oh? Am I intruding?"

Aly glared at him, the message on her face was, *Yes you are. Go jump in a lake!* But he wasn't looking at her, and Maude was assuring him shrilly, "Don't be silly. Have you eaten?"

"Not yet," he said. "But don't bother about me. I'll find something."

"There's chicken salad in a bowl," Merle offered.

There's rat poison on the top shelf, Aly declared telepathically. Unfortunately he was still only presenting her his rugged profile.

"Thanks," he shouted for the benefit of the older women.

"I'm bushed," Maude lamented, taking off her apron. "Merle and I are going to bed. See you kids tomorrow."

Before Aly could protest, she was alone in the kitchen with Rourk. His back was to her as he rummaged through the nearest refrigerator for something to eat.

Aly was hungry. She'd skipped lunch, and she'd only had a few bites of her sandwich. An urge to stalk out on him gnawed at her, but so did her stomach. She had to eat something. A thought struck her and she mumbled, "I think I'll finish this on the patio."

As she pushed through the door, he said, "Good idea. I'll join you."

She came to a crashing halt and whirled to face him. "Am I to assume you mean to shadow me, no matter where I go to eat?" she demanded.

He eyed her with true solemnity for the first time in a week. "Are you afraid to be alone with me?"

She swallowed, her silence answer enough.

His features darkened and he indicated the table with a curt nod. "Maybe we'd be better off eating in here rather than chance the provocative dangers of being alone together in the moonlight."

The remark conjured up unwanted images of naked flesh entwined and writhing under an August moon. Trying to quash the vision, she clutched her plate so hard she was surprised it didn't break in her fingers. "I have an idea," she said harshly. "Why don't you eat out there and I'll stay in here?"

"Or we could go into my bedroom and snack on each other."

He'd said it so softly it took a moment for the lewd suggestion to register. Yet it was hard to react with appropriate affront, considering their history.

Her heart went hammering into high gear, and her knees grew wobbly, but she tried to retain an unaffected facade. "You can be very crude, Mr. Rountree," she managed, though she'd sounded a bit breathy.

His lips quirked wickedly, as if to say, *I've heard you howl with passion because of my "crude" behavior, sweetheart.*

She felt a surge of defeat, and sighed, lowering her plate to the nearby countertop. They needed to talk rationally, get this said once and for all. Taking a seat at the table, she muttered, "Sit down, Rourk. Let's finish this."

His features closing in a curious frown, he did as she requested.

When he was seated next to her, she speared him with a direct look. "You're planning to make me pay for my lapse last week, aren't you?"

He watched her through half-lowered lids for a long while before saying anything. When he did, he spoke in a grave half growl. "Aly, control freaks are sick people—"

"Oh?" she shot back. "And from what curbside educational establishment did you get your degree in psychiatry?"

He pursed his lips through her rebuttal, then went on as though she hadn't interrupted. "And trying to be perfect is unhealthy."

She sniffed. "As opposed to trying to be the lowest life-form who can still walk upright?"

His fist hit the table hard, making Aly jump. "I want to help you, *dammit!*"

"You don't bear much resemblance to the American Red Cross," she threw back.

"I'm only saying you're trying too damned hard," he began again, more quietly. "You can't control everything merely by the strength of your will. Even the strongest of people are doomed to fail."

"As you did?" She lifted a recalcitrant chin. His expression registered pain, and she felt a twinge of remorse, but not enough to apologize.

"As I did," he murmured. Surprising her, he reached out and took her hand in his. "Aly, I like you. Being around you—your courage—has done something for me. I don't know.... I can't explain what."

"And you want to thank me by having sex with me, is that it?" she cut in, nervous and upset by the effect of his touch.

He scowled. "Would you mind just listening for a minute and quit judging?"

She bit her lower lip and gave him a single, stubborn nod.

Squeezing her fingers encouragingly, he said, "Anyway, my desire to help you seems to be pulling me out of my own black depression. I want to repay you for whatever it is you've done for me by offering you the wisdom of my experience."

Aly was having difficulty concentrating on his words. She was noting all too well her hand caught between both of his—a warm haven—and she found herself unable to draw her fingers away. "Because of you," he was saying, "I feel as though I might accomplish something—someday."

"Accomplish . . . what?" she asked slowly, dubiously.

He shrugged, and his indecisiveness gave her the power to yank from his hold. Vaulting to her feet, she set her face in determination. "You're welcome," she ground out. "And if sitting around thinking you *might* pull yourself together someday makes you feel like a man, then I'm tickled pink for you. But believe me, words don't mean much. Jack said that to me so many times it started making me sick to hear him say it."

For an instant she'd had a quiver of what? Hope? Hope that Rourk might have some backbone and turn out to be the kind of man she could love and respect? But, with his shrug, that hope was dashed. Gravely she exited the kitchen, able to conjure up only a bleak sort of dignity—like someone just sentenced to be shot at daybreak before a firing squad.

DAY BROKE WITH A LOT of noise, but no firing squad. It was just another day, a new day—a new beginning, Aly hoped. She put Rourke firmly from her thoughts as her hired crew tromped boisterously inside, ready to begin dismantling and moving heavy antiques to the grand ballroom in preparation for Saturday's auction. The crew consisted of three strapping ex-college-football-players-turned-gym-teachers who'd gone to high school with Aly: John, Mark, and Dave. The fourth crew member was Dave's younger brother, a nineteen-year-old named George, with mild Down's syndrome.

Aly was up at five, and had doughnuts and coffee ready for the crew at six-thirty. They ate like starving truck drivers, and laughed and teased Aly, calling her "boss." She was used to their ribbing. They'd helped on summer vacations, after school and weekends for years, and had always called her "boss" even when she hadn't been. Aly especially liked George. He teased little, smiled a lot, always pulled his weight, and was extremely appreciative of the opportunity to earn his way in the world.

It was just past two when Aly heard a sickening crash from Mrs. Rountree's bedroom. A second later, she heard George cry out, and the miserable wail riveted her with fright. She and Dave had been down the hall dismantling an eighteenth-century French chiffonier. Dave ground out a worried curse and struck out in a run. Getting control of herself, she dashed after him, praying the young man wasn't hurt.

When she rounded the doorjamb into the blue-and-beige bedroom, now devoid of anything but unadorned furniture, she saw George, crouched on his knees, trying to put pieces of clear cut-crystal back together into a shape that was now undeterminable. Small metallic gears and levers were also scattered around among sparkling shards of glass.

When she knelt beside George, she recognized the thing. It had once been a beautiful music box—not worth all that much compared to the bulk of the estate—maybe a thousand dollars—but for some reason, it had been one of the few things Rourk had cared enough about to keep.

"It was in the cabinet, Aly," John said, his tone miserable. "George was lifting it on the dolly and the door opened and the music box tumbled out."

"I didn't know anything was in it," George sobbed, shuddering with panic over the damage he'd done.

Aly's heart went out to the boy, and she put an arm about his quaking shoulders. "George," she whispered, trying to remain calm. "George, listen to me," she ordered softly, wiping away a tear from his cheek. "It wasn't your fault, George. Do you hear me? It was *my* fault. I left it in there by mistake."

George ran a fist under his nose. "But I broke it," he whimpered.

"No." She shook her head defiantly, feeling terrible about her neglect. But there were so many details, so much to do. How could she be expected to remember everything!

"No, George. This cabinet was supposed to be empty," she told him truthfully. "I forgot to pack it. You couldn't have known that music box was in there." She smiled at him, though realizing her expression was a weak one.

How was she ever going to tell Rourk about this? For a man who didn't give a damn about most things, he'd cared about this box. And now it was gone. She wanted to die, but she kept her expression encouraging and patted his rounded shoulder. "I'll clean it up, George. Why don't you and the guys go have a soft drink. It's time for a break, anyway."

George sniffled and stared at her. "You sure, boss?"

She nodded and rubbed his back affectionately. "Go on, George. And don't worry."

"Thanks, Aly," Dave murmured from above her left shoulder.

She looked up at him and nodded, assuring. "You know it wasn't George's fault, Dave."

He exhaled. "Look. I'm really sorry—"

"Take a break while I clean this up," she insisted. "We can get back to work on that chiffonier in fifteen minutes."

Dave nodded and the men shuffled out of the room. Aly began to pick up the valuable music-box fragments—or rather, they would have been valuable had they not been in several hundred spiky puzzle pieces.

A tremor of foreboding shook Aly's frame. What a *stupid* mistake for her to make. Leaving a precious keepsake in a cabinet like that. Even her father wouldn't have done anything so dumb.

Aly swallowed, trying to hold back mortified tears. Ahead of her loomed the dreadful obstacle of having to admit her failing to Mr. Rourk Rountree, the heir to this shattered, cherished music box.

"What am I going to tell him?" she whispered through a low moan.

"Why don't you try the truth," came a deep voice from behind her.

Aly jerked around, still on her knees, and in her haste, cut herself on a shard of broken crystal. Her wince of pain told Rourk what had happened.

"Dammit, Aly," he gritted, striding toward her. "Why do you always jump like a skittish kitten when I speak to you?"

"Maybe," she countered through pain-thinned lips, "because you're always coming up behind me."

"I remember coming up behind you once," he reminded less gruffly. "If you'll recall, you enjoyed every minute of it."

She'd been examining her knee, watching it leak blood. With his lurid reminder, she lifted narrowed eyes to scowl at him. "How gallant!" she retorted with cold sarcasm. "With my eyes closed I could almost mistake you for the Count of Monte Cristo."

The corners of his mouth twisted with annoyance, but he said nothing more as he knelt to take a closer look at the jagged cut on her knee. "*Hell.* Is it deep?"

"No. I'll take care of it."

Grasping her elbows, he pulled her to her feet. "Lean on me."

She was still holding several large pieces of the music box. Unsure what to do with them, she kept them as he gathered her to him and helped her to his mother's bathroom.

"Are there still bandages in here?"

She shook her head. "I cleaned everything out a couple of days ago."

"We can at least wash it," he said, leading her to the edge of the tub. "Sit. I'll take off your shoe."

"I can do it."

"Shut up, Aly." He pulled off her loafer. Turning on the water, he tested it for temperature, then commanded, "Stick your leg under the faucet."

She did as she was told. His black expression and sharp tone told her he had no intention of entering into a debate.

He ran water over her knee, his fingers directing the flow to gently cleanse her cut. She peered at his face as he worked. He looked unhappy, angry. Glancing down at her hand, still clutching the chunks of the music box, she realized why. He was aware of what she'd done. "Rourk," she began, her voice far from strong.

"What?" He didn't glance up from his work.

"Rourk, I have some bad news."

His hands stopped their ministrations, but remained in contact with her leg—a soft, intimate communion. When he turned, a hint of displeasure hovered in his gaze. "What now?" he asked tiredly. "I suppose Jack used to bathe your knees, and any male-knee contact makes you sick, too."

Disconcerted by his subdued reprimand, she looked away. "No . . . Actually, Jack hated the sight of blood. What I wanted to say was—" she forced herself to face him and tentatively held out the handful of shards "—I broke that music box you said you wanted to keep—"

"Yes, I can see that," he interrupted, frowning down at the sparkling pieces in her hand.

Taking them from her fingers he dumped them in a cardboard box that had been left behind for any final trash, then turned back to check her knee. "It's stopped bleeding," he told her, turning off the water.

As she watched in baffled silence, he shrugged out of his green knit shirt and began to blot her leg dry.

She pulled back. "Don't use your shirt, Rourk!" she cried.

"It's clean," he said, with a note of irritation.

"Please, Rourk." Taking the shirt from him, she folded it before handing it back to him. "Don't ruin a shirt for me. I broke a music box that was important to you. It doesn't matter that you have insurance. I've known you long enough to be aware that you don't care about much. I'm sorry. I screwed up. I forgot it was there." She ran a trembly hand through her spirally curls. "I know the insurance money isn't important to you. I wish it were. I wish it would buy you whatever that music box meant to you. I—I can't believe I let this happen. I—I—" She swallowed spasmodically. "I don't know how I could have made a mistake like that."

A flicker of some dark emotion crossed his face, and he stood to tower over her, a tense, frowning, half-naked man with all-too-alluring eyes.

"Aly," he began more softly than his scowling features would have suggested. "I saw how you handled George. It was damned compassionate. I'm afraid you have a chink in that control-freak armor of yours." He shook his head at her, mocking but without censure. "A year ago, I wouldn't have hired a boy like George. I'd have thought he would hamper productivity. I was a real ass." He was speaking very seriously, just above a whisper. "But you hired him, sweetheart. You may hate this coming from me, but I'd say there's hope for you, yet."

Aly had to strain to hear him as he went on, "I cared about that music box, because, once, a long time ago when I was in high school, it gave my mother happiness." He let out a caustic laugh. "Dad had forgotten her birthday, again. Was in Europe on another big deal.

So, I took all my savings, bought her the box and signed the card with Dad's name. Mother was thrilled." He half smiled, but the expression held more pain than happiness. "It wasn't until years later, I found out Mother knew all along that I'd gotten it for her. We'd both silently aided in perpetrating the fraud that my father gave a damn about either of us."

Aly was baffled, but didn't know what to say.

He shrugged wide shoulders. "It's probably just as well the music box is broken. It was part of the big lie I lived for too long, and that lie is finally over." He stopped, flexed his jaw several times, his eyes perusing her intently. "To hell with all music boxes. You know I don't give a damn about much. And if you want my honest opinion, you did anything *but* screw up back there. I told you before, you've given me something these past few weeks...." With a sage lift of one brow, as though he knew she'd interpret his remark in the worst possible way, he explained, "I don't mean your body, Aly. But don't discount how important that was to me." His regard glistened with sincerity as he murmured, "I'd like to give you something in return."

She swallowed, not sure she was understanding his meaning. "You're—sure you're not angry about the music box?"

He shook his head. "Only because it caused you pain." Reaching out, he touched her cheek with his knuckles, caressing slightly. His gaze tender, he promised, "Aly, I give you the freedom to be vulnerable. At least, around me."

As suddenly as his touch was gone, Rourk was gone. She could hear his receding footsteps as he left the bedroom and walked away from her down the hall.

Vulnerable? She frowned in confusion. He was offering her vulnerability?

Tentatively touching her cheek where his knuckles had stroked, she stared vacantly ahead. Vulnerability was out of the question, of course. She didn't dare be vulnerable, didn't dare let down her guard with Rourk. She had once, and it had led straight to bed. She couldn't allow that to happen again. Once more, and she might not be able to walk away from him.

Against her will, she had to admit his offer had been kind and wonderfully insightful. There seemed to be a great deal of gentleness in this man, and it frightened her to discover this sensitive side of his character.

The foolish, dangerously sentimental tear that escaped to slide down her cheek was mute testimony to how deeply his offer affected her. But no matter how tempting his proposal might be, no matter that he had a sensitive side, Rourk was *still* an idle bum who'd folded when life got too difficult, and Aly was still a woman in search of a solid, hardworking, steady—

With a low moan, she could no longer go on with her memorized litany. The gentle brush of Rourk's fist on her cheek, the honesty in his eyes, had done great damage to her life's plan. She shivered, terrified she was backsliding into another dead-end relationship.

Suddenly feeling as torn and shattered as the ruined music box, Aly burst into bewildered sobs.

9

THE MANSION'S GRAND ballroom was as quiet as a tomb and almost as dark, with only one wall sconce burning. Largely unfurnished to accommodate dancing, the room had a gaping, characterless flavor. Or perhaps it was just Aly's bleak state of mind and the lateness of the hour that made her view it that way.

All she was sure of was that she was too restless to try to sleep, though she'd been exhausted when her crew had gone home at eight o'clock. It was now after ten. Jenna was tucked in bed, and so were Maude and Merle.

Aly had spent the past two hours polishing her way through a fortune in antiques that she and her burly helpers had moved here and placed in rows that bordered three sides of the room. Now, rather than toss and turn in her lonely bed, she was laboring with grim determination, as though the future of the world depended on the quality of her reflection in each rich, hardwood surface.

She gave a last swipe to a cherry writing desk and moved on to polish frantically along the walnut case of a seventeenth-century Dutch grandfather clock. What a pity for her that it wasn't her reflection she was seeing in the deep wood grain. Instead of her smudged and harried features, she saw the face of a man, a face filled with dynamic vitality—from the ebony swath of hair falling across a broad forehead, the deep-set, bold eyes, noble aquiline nose, and sexy cleft chin, to that mouth, so resolute and masculine, yet generous and inviting.

She ground out an unladylike word and tried to rub the disquieting image out of both her mind and her heart.

"Evidently my offer this afternoon had no effect on you at all," a deep-pitched indictment echoed through the vast semidarkness.

Surprise siphoned the warmth from her face as she jerked around to see Rourk's massive silhouette framed in the open double entry. Because he was back-lit by faint light from an adjoining hallway, she couldn't make out his features. But his stance was painfully familiar as he lolled against the doorframe, the picture of rumpled indifference, both hands shoved in his hip pockets. His legs were crossed at the ankles, as though he'd been lounging there watching her for some time. A cigarette glowed red in front of his shadowed face.

With great effort, she pulled herself together. He'd crept up on her far too many times for her not to be growing accustomed to these unsettling visits. Still, her heart didn't slow to normal as quickly as she would have preferred.

Laying her polishing things on a convenient Chippendale commode, she faced him and called across the distance, "I suppose I should have expected this thief-in-the-night chat."

He drew himself upright and began to meander toward her. It was a disquieting drama—that graceful, manly stride—and she felt a throb of desire spring to life just witnessing his body move.

"You didn't come to dinner," he observed dryly, still advancing on her.

"I wasn't hungry," she lied, wondering why she felt as though she had to defend herself.

As he drew nearer, a flutter of unease swept through her. Why did she suddenly feel like some helpless quarry? Why did he seem like a wily predator? He was simply a rather muscular man in worn jeans, no socks, and a half-buttoned chambray shirt. There was nothing overtly predatory about that.

She swallowed, not believing a word of it. He was stalking her with more mesmerizing cunning than the most voracious jungle beast.

His cigarette tip glowed brightly, as though he'd taken a long drag. Then it went tumbling to the floor to be crushed beneath his heel.

"You should care more about your floor," she admonished, but her voice was thready and lacked authority.

"Why?" he scoffed, blowing out a long, thin stream of smoke as he came into the halo of light. "Is a perfect floor the high road to happiness?"

Aly sucked in a harsh breath to see his black, accusing glare. "What's wrong with *you?*" she demanded, upset. "Most clients don't get bent out of shape when we go to extra lengths to enhance their possessions for auction."

"I don't give a damn about 'enhanced possessions,' Aly, and you know it." He clenched his jaw, watching her with eyes narrowed in anger. "What do you plan to do? Drive yourself twenty-four hours a day? First you'll drive yourself crazy, then you start on everybody else. It's not a pretty future, sweetheart."

She took a defensive step away but the grandfather clock abruptly halted her backward movement. Bumping into the clock jarred its mechanism and its innards jangled, giving away her intentions. Frustrated anger shot through her, but that quickly mutated into renewed determination. She wouldn't be intimidated by this man any longer.

"I've been thinking about what you said this afternoon," she shot back, her voice tense. "What you said about George and a chink in my armor." She paused. Rourk scowled, but kept quiet, so she forged on, "I *hate* to disappoint you, but there's no chink in my armor. George can do the work. It's as simple as that." She glared at him, but there was a wariness in her tone she hoped he couldn't detect. "I wouldn't have hired him if I didn't know he could do the job. I couldn't afford to. So," she challenged, "what do you have to say to that?"

He grinned sardonically. "It took you all afternoon to rationalize yourself out of being an admirable human into some kind of fledgling company hard-nose?" He shook his head, muttering, "Congratulations. But don't think you fool me, Aly, because you're dealing with an ex-pro hard-nose, here. I'm a man who actually fired a woman when I found out she was pregnant." He snorted in self-disgust. "Of course, I called it an economic-turndown layoff."

His harsh confession startled her and she faltered. "But—I . . ."

"I dare you to fire George," he cut in. "Tell him not to come back, tomorrow. Then, maybe I'll put you up for membership in the *real* hard-nose club." He eyed her steadily, his voice dropping to a guttural, rough register. "But the dues are high, sweetheart. Damned high . . ."

Disconcerted, she pointedly turned away. "Don't you kid yourself, Mr. Rountree. You haven't lost your talent for being a hard-nosed jerk. You made me cry to-day—" She stilled, horrified that she'd let that slip.

"Why did you cry?" he asked, sounding nearer.

She felt impaled by his scrutiny and shook her head, not trusting her voice.

"Damn it," he ground out. "Why did my offer make you cry?"

"Because!" she spat, working hard at keeping reins on her frayed control. "Vulnerability is a tempting but expensive weakness. I can't afford it—"

"It's not a matter of 'can't,' Aly," he interrupted. "You must allow yourself to be vulnerable. Too much control kills your ability to feel."

"I've felt quite enough in my life, thank you!" she objected. "I've felt helplessness and I've felt—felt the back of a man's hand—" Her voice broke.

He turned her abruptly to face him, dragging her into his arms. "I never wanted to make you cry, Aly. I care about you."

Before she'd found the wit to respond, his mouth hungrily covered hers. Fighting her need for him—her desire to be exactly where she was—she pushed away with all her might, whimpering, "Your kisses make me so vulnerable, I—"

"And yours make me strong, Aly," he broke in hoarsely, his lips brushing hers. "When I hold you, I can do anything...."

He took possession of her mouth again, his strength of purpose so galvanizing it sent her resolve spinning off into the void of good-intentions-gone-awry. Against her will, her arms flung themselves about his neck, and she took everything he had to give, giving everything she had in return. Lost. Lost again—completely vulnerable—in the dizzying persuasion of his lovemaking.

Aly had no idea how she got there, but when she next came to her senses—at least partially—she was reclining on her back, stark naked, in Rourk's bed. Snuggling more intimately in his arms, the afterglow of wonderful sex still had her body tingling.

Pleasantly drugged by his kisses, she turned toward him and began to nibble at the contours of his broad chest, slipping her arms about him and sighing with satisfaction. She was aware that there was a hint of poignancy in that sigh, but it was so faint she didn't think Rourk would detect it.

Hours ago, back in the ballroom, she'd given in to him again. She supposed her weakness for Rourk was similar to an alcoholic's weakness for booze. She'd heard it said that an alcoholic takes the first drink, then that first drink drinks the rest—the point being, don't take that first drink.

Rourk was her addiction. She could stay sober and straight as long as he didn't press his mouth to hers. But as soon as those knowing lips found their mark, she was like a drunk on a bender. Lost-weekend time. In her case she should spell it w-e-a-k-e-n-d.

Dejected laughter gurgled in her throat at the pun. *Weak end.* And unfortunately, the weak end wasn't behind her—that is, over yet, for Rourk's fingers were plying their expert trade, working sensual magic between her thighs, setting her body to humming again.

"What's funny?" he asked in a love-thickened whisper.

"Not—a—thing," she admitted through a breathy sigh, meaning it. There was nothing funny at all about their relationship. It was really very sad that she was such a soft touch where this man's sexual prowess was concerned. His fingers set her throbbing, and she gasped.

Attuned to recognize the signs of her ultimate surrender, Rourk applied protection and slid over her. She spread her legs in wanton, welcome compliance. "Oh . . . Rourk," she groaned, trying to be true to herself, to her life's plan. "This has to be the last time—"

His only response was to thrust and thrust again, making her cry out and claw lovingly at his back.

Much later, spent to the tips of her toes, and thoroughly sated, Aly lay wide-eyed, staring into the darkness. The bedside clock registered the hour in a garish fluorescent green. It was four in the morning. Rourk had been asleep for a long time, but he still held her possessively to him. She feared trying to leave. If she did, she'd only awaken him and he'd pull her back into his embrace, kiss her soundly, and she'd forsake her convictions once more.

She released a long, low exhale, then bit her lip at the loudness of the unhappy sound in the still night.

"Why the sigh?" Rourk murmured, grazing her ear with his lips.

She blinked, startled, and turned slightly to face him. "I didn't know you were awake," she whispered, stalling for time and for an answer that would get her out of there without a fight.

"I was thinking," he said, his tongue and lips teasing the tip of her nose.

She swallowed. She had to leave soon. She could already feel herself falling under his erotic spell. "Rourk . . . It's so late. . . ."

"Don't you want to know what I've been thinking about?" he said, smoothing a tendril of hair from her cheek and replacing it with a moist kiss.

She closed her eyes, relishing his mouth against her skin. "Okay. What have you been thinking about?" she asked through a wayward smile.

His teeth grazed the rise of her breast, nipping lightly as he murmured, "I love you, Aly. And I've been wondering what to do about it."

Her eyes went platter-wide, and she stiffened. "What?" she asked, not trusting her hearing.

"I said," he settled lingering kisses lower and lower as he repeated softly, "I love you. I don't think I've ever really loved a woman before you."

Catching her breath, she pressed lightly against his chest. She was taking this news very peculiarly. Her heart was thrilling with wonder and womanly delight, but her eyes were blurring with tears—desperate, unhappy tears.

"Oh, Rourk . . ." she murmured fearfully, but her objection was cut short by his lips taking full, wildly satisfying possession of hers.

"Rourk, please . . ." she whimpered, when he lifted his mouth enough to allow her to respond. "Don't do this to me. . . ."

She pressed more firmly, but not as firmly as her agony demanded. He held a great physical and mental power over her that was hard to fight, especially when lying naked against him.

With enormous determination, she managed to back away from his hold, though he instinctively reached for her, taking her hand. "What's wrong?" he demanded, coming up on one elbow. "You're not going to tell me you don't have some feeling for me. Not after what we've shared."

His expression was dear, compelling. Even in the darkness, she could see the glisten of honest concern in his eyes. Her mouth worked as she floundered for a way to explain how she felt—a way not to hurt him—but she couldn't find the right words.

"Aly," he coaxed, tugging her gently toward him. "Come back under the covers."

His husky tone told her he had sexy surprises in store, and part of her begged to be returned to the seductive refuge of his body and his bed, but she resisted, belatedly tugging from his warm grasp.

"I can't . . ." she mourned brokenly.

"Yes, you can, sweetheart," he crooned, stroking her thigh, so very sure of his influence over her.

She felt the pull of his sensuality and flushed, lurching desperately from the bed with a despondent wail. "No! Rourk, I've told you how it is with me so many times! Nothing's changed!"

He followed her, taking her in his arms and crushing her to him. "Things have changed," he insisted, his voice low and resolute. "We love each other, damn it!"

"No!" she protested. But as soon as the denial was out of her mouth, she realized what a blatant lie it was. "No..." she repeated, but this time with a tinge of awe, of disbelief. She couldn't be in love with Rourk Rountree. *He wasn't what she wanted in a man!*

"Rourk, we can't love each other. It won't work," she said sadly. "You don't care about anything. I'd nag at you and you'd grow to hate me for it."

He laughed, but without mirth. "I'm a millionaire, Aly. We can lie around and make love all day if we want."

"That's your ambition?" she asked, disappointed to the point of tears. "*Damn you*, Rourk. I'd eat glass before I'd spend one more day in a relationship with a man who's only game plan is to play hard, dream big and drift aimlessly through life!" Fear and rage were knotted together, tying up her insides. "You'll run through your millions in a couple of years. Then what? I'll tell you what," she accused, on the edge of sobbing. "You'll be restless, unfulfilled and angry at the world and you'll start taking it out on me and Jenna!"

"Not all men are asses like your ex," he objected gravely, reaching for her, but she deftly avoided his touch.

"Maybe. But you haven't shown me where you're much different," she cried. "Don't you have *any* ambition, any drive?"

His brows drew together in a tormented expression. "Ambition and drive are what got me where I am today," he reminded her, his tone biting.

"Oh, Rourk," she flared, tired of his excuses for his weakness. "I know, I know. So you ran your company with an iron fist, so you worked twenty-four hours a day and neglected your wife, so she left you and took your baby and you fell apart and became a directionless vagabond. You toured the world to lick your wounds, then you came home to pout." Her distress grew almost overwhelming when she found she couldn't keep her hands from shaking.

Clenching her fingers into tight knots, she tried more quietly, "Rourk, I have to respect the man I love. I *have to*, or I can't—can't have a relationship with him. I admit that some horrible flaw in me has made me fall in lo—" She stuttered to a halt, upset that she'd even partially admitted it aloud. Blundering on, she amended,

"But this 'thing' can't go any further. To be blunt, I—I *don't like* you!"

He flinched as though he'd been punched. "This thing?" he repeated, his voice going empty and cold.

Feeling his suffering all too clearly, her body went as insubstantial as jelly, but she forced herself to lift her chin, to face his icy gaze. But that was as far as her bravado would take her. She didn't have the heart to conjure up hateful words that would give him more grief.

After a deadly pause, he nodded solemnly and said, "I see." Plainly trying to contain his temper, he added, "I also see why your husband drank. You have a lethal bedside manner," he accused, a thin chill hanging on his words.

Aly gasped at his verbal slap. "How dare—"

"You tell a man you love him, then you kick him in the teeth," he ground out, his expression brooking no argument. "But let's be clear on one thing. My wife didn't run away. She and my daughter—died." His nostrils flared as he uttered the ugly word as though he'd never said it aloud until this minute. His features hardening further, he growled, "I was busy, as usual, and I sent Megan and the baby on vacation in our private jet without me. Said I'd join her in a couple of days. She was crying when I hung up." He stopped, clearing his throat. The words seemed to be coming very hard. "You see, I had an urgent meeting and she didn't want to be sent off alone, but I insisted. It had happened a few times before, but I knew we'd have years to be together. One more little womanly fit of tears wasn't important."

With a caustic flash of teeth, he said bitterly, "After all, I was a man with ambition and drive." He closed his eyes for a moment before his foul curse broke the desolate stillness, making Aly jump. "Three hours later, my family was dead. Wind shears. My last memory of my wife . . . was her tears." His suffering and guilt lay naked in his eyes as he whispered harshly, "I'd been a bastard once too often. . . ."

Intense desolation swept through Aly. "I—I didn't know . . ." she whispered, her voice fragile.

He'd averted his gaze, but her words pulled him back. "Go ahead and say it. Tell me I treated them more like possessions than people I was supposed to love. Megan did." His voice had gone raspy, each word wrenched out as though from an open wound. "She also told me a woman needs a flesh-and-blood man for a husband, not a stainless-steel knight-errant." He laughed, the sound grating and forlorn. "I'd tried to be the best at everything I did for so many years—conquering, defeating, winning—I forgot how to simply be a human being.

"Don't make my mistake, Aly." His tone grew somber, yet was knife-sharp. "It's a sickly substitute for living."

"You must have had a reason—I mean, for being that way," she retorted, wanting him to face the fact that there were perfectly legitimate motivations for trying to be in control of one's life.

"Yeah," he snorted. "I wanted my damned father to notice me—between international business deals. I figured if I got awards, he'd make an effort to come to at least some of the ceremonies."

Aly was taken aback by the animosity in his tone, but didn't interrupt. "Then it became a habit," he said. "Finally, the more control I had, the more I wanted. Power is an addictive aphrodisiac, Aly. The irony is that ultimately instead of having control, it has you, consuming the human in you like a malignancy, and suddenly there's nothing real, nothing loving, nothing left inside your skin but a power-crazed monster."

"You make it sound so cut-and-dried awful," she objected. "But it's not that way with me. I just refuse to ever be controlled again—especially by a self-centered, weak man. Besides, my family needs—"

"Aly," he cut in more gently, "no matter what you may think of my life-style, I don't want to control you."

"Oh, no?" She choked out a disbelieving laugh. "You've been trying to change me practically since we met, telling me I'm so wrong." She tossed her head defiantly. "If you profess to love me, then why can't you love me as I am?"

A dark brow arched dubiously. "I could ask you the same question."

She bristled. He had a point, but she'd told him from the first she couldn't abide his type. Just because she was having some sort of unfortunate, temporary, attraction to him didn't change that. Running a distracted hand through her tangled hair, she said, "Don't you see? I won't settle just because I have this—this thing for you." His jaw tightened ominously at her word choice, but she hurried on. "It's like the old saying, 'You can fall in love with a rich man as easily as a poor one.' Well, I figure I can fall in love with a strong, hard-working man as easily as a weak, shiftless one."

His closed features mirroring his offense, he snarled, "If you're looking for strong and hardworking, I could fix you up with a tractor I know."

She heaved such an overwrought moan it sounded like a curse. "Why can't you take me seriously!"

"You're the one who wants to be a plaster saint. Don't ask me to worship at your shrine."

Offended and fighting tears, she demanded, "What's so wrong with my trying to avoid making big mistakes in my life?"

"And you think loving me would be a big mistake?" The remark was harsh, half questioning, half challenging.

She shot him a cold look. He stood before her so boldly handsome, yet so vulnerable in his naked fury that it was hard for her to keep her strength of will. Granted, he'd had a worse tragedy in his life than Jack. Granted, he had a sensitive side and didn't really seem to be inclined toward violence. But, the very point was, Rourk didn't seem to be inclined toward *anything*. He was a complete burnout case. Aly couldn't allow herself to be saddled with that, either. No matter what her heart might crave. She already had enough responsibilities!

Deep sobs of regret racked her insides, but she tried to keep her face composed. She loved a man who was no good for her. *Again.* She'd fought her attraction and lost. But if she could be strong—stay away from him and his damnable kisses, for two more weeks—she'd be out of his life and free to find the respectable, hardworking kind of man she needed. Tears of frustration and remorse trembling on her eyelids, she whispered tightly, "Yes . . . Rourk. Loving you would be a very big mistake."

His cobalt eyes sparked with furious lightning. "Okay, sweetheart," he retorted. "But think about this. The crap we promise ourselves in our darkest moments is the very crap that keeps us in the dark."

She shook her head in denial, but he cut across her attempt to rebuke him. "You go on trying to be as perfect as God. But this isn't over," he warned, his tone as firm and final as death.

In a surprise move, he reached out and stroked her breast. She started at the unexpected intimacy and staggered a step away, but her unsteady intake of breath revealed things she didn't want him to know about the effect he had on her.

His malevolent chuckle grated, and the twisted grin he flashed was perverse, though his eyes were full of wrath and determination rather than any glint of humor. In one forward motion he pulled her into his arms, his lips teasing hers. "If loving me makes you flawed and human," he vowed, "then I'm hot for the idea, understand?" With one hand on her hip, he pressed her firmly into his erection, pledging roughly, "And, babe, when it's all said and done—you'll be hot for it, too."

Aly's heart plummeted to her feet. Hearing such an insolent prophecy while clasped so lewdly to him was devastating to her peace of mind, and yet, some wayward part of her thrilled to the idea.

All too conscious of where his flesh touched hers, Aly's being cried out to wrap her legs around his hips in wild, mindless abandonment. She was slipping fast. But she was also very angry—angry that he thought he had such effortless physical control over her. Never again would a man have her bending to his whim, whether it was brutally or gently demanded. The next man she loved, *she* would choose! *End of debate*.

Her indignation barely won out, and she recovered her shaky resolve, pushing hard against him. "No—no—" she whimpered desperately, backing away. "I'm through being weak for weak men!" To her amazement, he didn't resist, but allowed her her freedom, unhindered.

She cast a furtive glance at his face. The corner of his mouth was twisted with savage annoyance, his down-drawn features a withering scowl, but he said nothing, made no further move to stop her. He just watched her with hooded, riveting eyes.

Not wanting him to witness the mixture of emotions on her face, she spun away and darted from his bedroom. It wasn't until she was a whole floor above him that she realized she was naked. Shuffling to a shocked halt, she sagged against the cool, papered wall to thank heaven it was the middle of the night. Maude and Merle might not hear well, but they could see just fine, and they wouldn't have let her nude hall-scampering pass without a very loud, very humiliating inquisition.

10

"WHAT DO YOU MEAN, the chairs are lost?" Aly cried in a loud-enough voice for her mother to hear. "How can anybody lose five hundred chairs?"

Maude shrugged, clamping her hand over the phone's receiver. "The rental-store manager said the truck started out with the chairs and display tables at one o'clock. That was over two hours ago."

This was the last straw! Aly groaned. "Tell him we *have* to have those chairs. No excuses. The preview's tonight and we've got to have everything ready by six-thirty."

Maude turned away to screech into the phone.

"Aly?" Dave asked, sounding cautious. "Where'd you want us to set up that Victorian bed frame?"

She ran both hands through her tumble of hair. "Oh, I don't know. Just lean the headboard and footboards up against the wall near the far window. There won't be enough room for you to reassemble it in here."

Dave nodded and trotted off just as Mike yelled, "Aly! That damn broken lock's frozen up again. We can't open the door so we can get the rest of that Chippendale stuff."

Aly had a pounding headache, and the fact that nothing was going right didn't help. Nothing had gone right for three days. Not to mention the fact that she hadn't slept a wink. Rourk had prowled silently through the mansion, his eyes sparking with a disturbing message. And when they'd been forced to speak, he'd grinned in that sardonic way that made her go limp. No soft, coaxing words, no hint of seduction. In those long, sleepless hours, she'd decided he must be trying reverse psychology on her, playing hard-to-get to force her to realize she couldn't give him up. Well, Mr. Irresistible Rountree could play hard-to-get until—until Arnold Schwarzenegger sang "I Am Woman," for all she cared. His sneaky ploy would do him no good.

"*Aly?*" Mike repeated. "What about that lock?"

Yanked back to her crisis of the moment, she made a guttural sound of frustration, and shouted, "Handle it, Mike! That's what I'm paying you for. Take the hinges off if you have to."

He frowned, nodded and sprinted off.

Movement caught her eye and she grimaced, "No, George. Put those smaller pieces in *front*."

"In front of what, boss?" George asked, perplexed.

Aly's head hurt so badly it was painful to even shift her gaze. Rubbing the bridge of her nose she called tiredly, "In front of the bigger pieces. So the people will be able to see them." Noting his continued squint of confusion, she hurried across the large room and pointed out where he was to place the splay-legged table he was holding. "Start another row here for the little stuff."

George carefully lowered the table, looking subdued as he walked off. Aly frowned. Had she yelled at him? She hadn't meant to. It must be the headache.

"*Sieg Heil*, sweetheart," came a mocking salutation from behind her.

Aly closed her eyes and massaged her throbbing temples. She could pretend indifference every bit as well as he. Rourk had made a point of taking her to task for every little thing the past three days, pointing out to her in subtle ways how she never eased up, never laughed or joked or took a break. She wanted to scream!

Today, he was having a field day. She'd become a raging shrew and she knew it. But there would be several hundred people ambling through here tonight between seven and ten o'clock to get a look at what was being auctioned tomorrow, and she didn't even have all the furniture set up yet. And now the chairs were lost somewhere. Probably being erected in some startled couple's backyard.

She reluctantly turned to confront Rourk, her face set to hide her inner turmoil. "Look, why don't you go to a bar and pick a fight with a truck driver. I don't have time right now."

"It's a charming thought," he responded dryly. "But I'm here to deliver a message from Merle."

She shot a glance to the opposite corner of the room where her aunt was stacking boxes. "Why did she send you?"

"Have you taken any aspirin for that headache?"

"How did you know I have a headache?"

He shook his head at her. "Let me put it this way. Miss Congeniality, you're not."

She couldn't really argue with that, and her head hurt too much to fight. With a pained sigh, she asked, "So, why did my aunt send *you* with her message? Doesn't she think I have enough trouble?"

His lips curved derisively. "I think she figures if you kill the messenger, she'd rather it be me than her."

Aly felt as though he'd pulled a plug and she was deflating. "What now?" she exhaled tiredly.

"Jenna threw up."

"Oh, Lord. Why didn't you tell me!" Aly headed for the playpen that had been set up near where her aunt was working.

"I don't think it's anything Merle couldn't handle, Aly," Rourk said, following her.

"I'd better check," she mumbled more to herself than anyone else, as she hurried to her daughter. "What is it, Aunt Merle?"

Jenna was standing up, chattering away, her face and playsuit soiled. Aly felt her forehead. "She doesn't feel hot."

Merle shrugged, ripping packing tape off one of the boxes. "Could be she just had a gas bubble."

"I'd better clean her up," Aly muttered.

"Chairs are here!" Maude shouted from the door.

"Finally!" Aly felt a surge of relief, but didn't quite smile. Looking around, she asked, "Where's John?"

"You sent him to get more light bulbs for the turntable," Merle reminded at the top of her lungs.

"Oh, right." Aly had lifted her messy daughter and grew confused about what to handle first. "Can you handle Jenna?"

"I guess. But somebody has to set up those tables for all this cut glass."

"Oh, I forgot we were going to get rid of that at this auction. Never mind."

"Where do you want the chairs?" yelled a burly deliveryman.

"It's about time!" shouted Aly.

"Look, lady," the man complained. "I ain't had such a good day, either. So stay off my case."

Aly bristled. She'd had just about enough grief for one day. Hiking up her daughter, she marched over to the man and said, "Listen, we're paying for five hundred chairs and four display tables, not a lecture. So bring the chairs in and save your gripes for Oprah."

The man caught sight of Jenna and made a sour face. "Yuck. What's wrong with him?"

"Her," Aly corrected as calmly as she could. "Never mind that. You're two hours late. Start getting them set up."

"Lady, I don't get paid to set up. I'm leavin' 'em in the drive."

Aly opened her mouth to protest, but was surprised when Rourk stepped in. "Hey, man . . ." With a casual arm slung about the burly fellow's shoulder, he led him away, suggesting, "Let's give the lady a break and bring them inside. You were two hours late, remember? Or, we could check with your boss if you'd like."

Aly stared after them. She had the oddest feeling there'd been a threatening note in Rourk's voice. She wondered if the chair-rental man, shorter by almost a foot than Rourk, had heard it, too, or if it had only been her overwrought imagination.

Apparently the man had detected something. By the time Aly had changed Jenna, the chairs were stacked in the foyer and the truck was gone. Aly stumbled to a disbelieving halt to see Rourk helping Dave set up the chairs in the ballroom. Unable to do more than gape, she followed his progress as he passed by on his way for another batch. He looked rugged, lean and vaguely amused.

"Close your mouth, Aly. Bugs will get in," he said with a wry grin.

Finding her voice, she demanded, "What are *you* doing?"

"How's Jenna?" he asked, turning to face her.

"Fine. But what—"

"Did you take some aspirin?" he cut in.

"Yes, yes! But, what are you doing?"

He indicated Dave, George and Mark with a nod. "You've got these poor, defenseless men scared out of their wits. I thought I'd better lend a hand before you made one of them cry."

"Very funny," she quipped, finding it strangely difficult to remain upset with this man. His eyes twinkled, and he seemed so—so pleasant, she had an urge to smile, but pricked pride made her squelch it. "For your information, Mr. Rountree, the way you handled the deliveryman wasn't exactly how Mother Teresa would have done it."

He lifted a brow in pretended confusion.

"Don't act so innocent," she countered. "I could hear your if-you-want-to-leave-with-all-your-teeth-you'll-do-what-I-say tone."

His sudden grin flashed with eroticism, doing strange things to her. "I'm a backsliding bastard. Sorry," he said, not sounding a bit apologetic.

Before Aly had time to agree with his assessment, Rourk turned away and went back to work.

She couldn't resist covertly watching him, but a wariness slithered up her spine. What was his game? He'd baited her, teased her and when it suited him, ignored her, since their last—midnight—encounter. She'd thought it was reverse psychology. But, if that was the case, then what was this new twist? Why was he suddenly being so helpful?

Not wanting to dwell on his motives, she turned back to her job. But try as she would to ignore him, she found herself gazing in his direction as he strolled by with another load of chairs. He was strong, she had to give him that. And well put-together. Most definitely an enigma.

She shook her head in consternation. As soon as she thought she had him figured, he did something to shatter her image of him. There were moments when she almost liked him, and whole days she utterly detested him. Unfortunately, three nights ago she'd discovered that even on the days she detested him, she was still hopelessly drawn to him—

"Aly!" Merle squealed. "Since you want the cut glass to be displayed from the door along the wall to the windows, I can't start setting these tables with glass until the chairs are all in. They might brush a table edge and knock over some of the pieces."

Aly nodded in reluctant agreement. "Okay. To hurry things up, let's move some chairs in, then I'll help with the setup."

"*Hell*, Aly!" Mike roared from the ballroom entry. "That damn door— We took off its hinges, and it toppled sideways on your mother."

Aly's eyes widened in horror, but he waved it off with a dismissive hand, saying, "She's not hurt. A big box of dishes she was marking took most of the punishment." He screwed up his face, his expression one of nervous misgivings. "Sounded like—uh—a little breakage in the box, though," he added warily.

Aly closed her eyes and groaned, wondering if this horrible day would ever end.

ODDLY ENOUGH, THE PREVIEW went smoothly. Now, at ten-thirty, Aly and John were sitting in the kitchen relaxing over coffee. Dave, Mike and George had gone home. Jenna was asleep and Maude and Merle had retired to their rooms. Aly had no idea where Rourk was. She tried to tell herself she didn't care.

Aly undid the top button of her white blouse and suggested, "Loosen your tie, John. It's been a long day."

At five o'clock the men had finished setting up the room, and had gone home to change into black slacks, white dress shirts and black ties. Merle, Maude and Aly wore black skirts and white blouses—their official auction attire. Now that the preliminary viewing was over, her clothes seemed constrictive and uncomfortable.

John tugged at the knot in his tie and grinned. Aly grinned back. John was a nice man with boyish good looks. With dark-blond hair, rather John Ritter-like features, he was almost six feet tall and husky. Divorced, no kids. For a long time he'd been putting out vibes that he was interested in a relationship, but she had mixed feelings about it. True, he was a hard worker, easygoing, good with Jenna, and taught physical education at one of Wichita's middle schools. Even so, Aly hadn't been able to conjure up much excitement for the idea of dating him. And especially now, considering her ambivalent feelings about Rourk.

But she had the feeling John was working up to asking her out. Maybe she should give him a chance. With an encouraging smile, she took another sip of her coffee.

"Aly," he began quietly. "I was wondering if you—"

"Am I interrupting?" came a gratingly familiar voice. "Smelled the coffee and couldn't resist."

Aly cast Rourk a troubled look as he strolled into the kitchen. His eyes sparkled devilishly, as though he knew exactly what he was thwarting by popping in. She had an urge to jump him and ring his neck. Or at least she hoped that was what her urge involved.

"You're not interrupting a thing," John said, sounding wistful.

Rourk got himself a mug and filled it. "Good crowd tonight. Don't you think?"

"About what we expected," Aly mumbled into her cup's rim.

"I have to admit," Rourk offered jovially, propping his feet on the table and leaning precariously back in his chair, "you folks managed to pull everything together."

"Thank you," Aly demurred, worried that he planned to say something personal and embarrass her in front of John. When he said nothing more, she began to relax a little.

The silence started to drag. Not knowing what else to do, Aly shifted her gaze to John and asked, "What were you talking about before?"

He looked sheepish. "Well, I was thinking—" He took a sip of his coffee and licked his lips. It suddenly hit Aly what he'd been about to say before Rourk had come in and scrambled her brains. She flinched, realizing she'd put John in the difficult position of asking her out in front of a witness. Well, if he decided to go through with it, she certainly had no intention of embarrassing him further by refusing.

"I was wondering," he went on, his expression somber, his eyes almost pitifully anxious, "if you'd like to go see that new Jeff Bridges picture with me after the auction tomorrow."

Her resolve faltered, and so did the smile she'd plastered on. Tomorrow after the auction they had to get things cleaned up and ready for Sunday's jewelry disposal. Of course, there wouldn't be nearly as much heavy work. The rental stuff was already set up, though the jewelry sale would require some rearranging. Still, it wouldn't be that strenuous a day. And because the jewelry wouldn't be on the premises until the day of the auction—for security purposes—the only preview would be for an hour and a half before the bidding began. Deciding she could honor her silent pledge to say yes, she nodded. "I'd love to."

John brightened. "And dinner first?"

Aly paused. "I guess . . . Sure. Tomorrow's auction should be over by three. Cleanup and rearranging will take until five." She toyed with her cup. "Pick me up at seven?"

"Well . . . Great!" John said, beaming. His chair scraped the floor as he stood. "I'd probably better go now. See you at eight sharp in the morning."

Aly stood, too, casting Rourk a stealthy but intensely curious look beneath her lashes. He appeared to be a thousand miles away, sipping his coffee and staring out over the rim of his mug. She experienced an odd surge of dismay. What had she expected him to do? Roundly refuse to allow her to date another man? Why? Just because they'd spent two nights together having wildly satisfying sex, and just because he'd professed to be in love with her? He'd made it clear over the past several weeks that he didn't care much about anything, but for some reason, she'd thought he'd been fairly earnest about that, at least.

She tried to shrug off her feeling of heaviness. With counterfeit gaiety, she offered, "I'll walk you to the door, John." Coming around the table, she determinedly took his arm. To heck with Rourk's opinion—whatever it might be. He certainly gave no hints by the look on his impassive face. If *he* didn't care, *she* certainly didn't!

Fifteen minutes later, John was gone. Aly knew she didn't have to go back into the kitchen. Her mug would survive through the night unwashed, and Rourk would no doubt unplug the coffeepot. But some impulse compelled her to retrace her steps.

John had kept Aly at the door droning on about current trends in weather and politics. Aly had tried to act interested. Then, when conversation hit a lull, he'd lightly kissed her lips. She'd flushed with surprise, but she hadn't gone all light-headed. Darn! Why was it necessary that she go silly when a man kissed her? John was perfect for her, so why was she trekking back to the painfully *imperfect* Rourk? And why was she hungering for him to take her into his arms?

Her heart hammered in anticipation. If he glanced at her just once with that soft, loving grin, she'd give in; and drat it, she *wanted* to give in! She missed his kisses, missed the warmth that hovered in his eyes when they lay in each other's arms. And she missed the sexy words he whispered when she was on the brink of climax. Recalling everything set her glowing with yearning and expectancy, and she couldn't suppress a small smile— didn't even want to—remembering the nights they'd spent together.

Pushing in the kitchen door, she opened her mouth to speak, but found herself stumbling to a halt—alone. The coffeemaker was unplugged and the pot rinsed out. Three mugs sat upside down on a clean dish towel next to the sink. As she gazed around the empty room, her smiled faded. Somehow, it seemed emptier and lonelier than ever.

THE AUCTION STARTED promptly at nine-thirty. Maude registered people as they came in, assigning bidder's numbers. Aly had taken over as full-time auctioneer since her father's death. And Merle, who didn't like to handle money, was official clerk, taking a position at the podium beside Aly, writing down who bought what and at what price.

The turntable was three feet around and divided in its center by a high, satin-draped partition, so that while one item was being auctioned, another could be set up on the backside. To enhance the look of the items, the turntable top was glass, and lights shone up through the base for dramatic effect.

It was now after eleven in the morning. The cut-glass portion of the auction was drawing to a close. Aly had been chanting constantly for almost two hours. At twelve, they would have a five-minute break. It wasn't much time, but the auction business was fast-paced and no-nonsense. There were few frills.

An exquisite English cut-amethyst bowl was turned toward the audience and Aly started the bidding at five hundred dollars. Up went a hand. Her wireless mike carried her auctioneer's chant easily across the big room. She had long ago learned to move through the process without effort.

She remembered watching her father as a young girl—then helping him by standing on the other side of the turntable, mimicking his arm movements. Maude always laughed and said the two of them looked like they were involved in some upper-body kung-fu exercise.

Today, George—all starched and spiffy—had surprised her by matching her movements as she had once helped her father, so that those on the far side the room could better follow the bidding. His efforts were quite good, Aly thought. Though he'd been a regular participant in their sales for the past five years, she'd never realized he'd been absorbing so much.

The easy flow of their harmonized motions was magnetic in its own way. Aly had been told more than once, by people who hadn't attended an auction before, that watching the hypnotic dance of the auctioneer and his or her assistant was fascinating, almost sensual.

The bidding stalled at two thousand dollars. She chanted out the rapid, sonorous cadence, "Going-going-gone-for-two-thousand-dollars-to-number-twenty-three." Both she and George accomplished their final swirl and point in startling unison.

Then John, in a white shirt, charcoal tie and slacks, took the bowl off the turntable and trekked it out to the person holding up bidder number twenty-three. As Merle wrote the information down, the turntable revolved to display a set of twelve perfect wine goblets, glinting and winking in the upsurge of light.

Out of the corner of her eye, Aly noticed someone come to the ballroom entryway—the darkly clad figure of a man, tall and powerful. She glanced toward the back of the room, already starkly aware of his identity.

Rourk was at last making an appearance. He looked casually elegant in black wash slacks and a snug black polo shirt. As usual, he wore no socks.

At most auctions, owners of the collections being sold were ardently interested in the proceedings, some even wrote down every penny bid. But, Rourk, it appeared, cared as little about this aspect of his life as he did any other.

Their eyes met, and he nodded curtly, but didn't smile. He simply lounged there, hands thrust into his front pockets.

Taking a sip of water, Aly tried to ease the sudden dryness that had crept into her throat before beginning her new chant, this time asking for an opening price of six hundred dollars.

She forced her mind to business, moving through the bids with precise, football/referee-type movements, to and fro, in and out, while George duplicated her actions amazingly well for someone who had never done it publicly before. She wondered if he had dreams of being an auctioneer, and had practiced in front of his mirror at home. Sweet kid.

The bidding escalated quickly, for the dozen goblets were among the most valuable items listed in the catalog. Just as an offer of fifteen-hundred and fifty dollars was made, a gruff voice boomed out over the loudspeakers, proposing lewdly, "Hey, Dirty Mama, come on!" There was a spat of static, then, "Dirty Mama, this is Lover Buddy. You read? Come on!"

Aly bit her lip. On rare occasions, shortwave radios interfered with their sound system, and there was nothing they could do but wait it out. With a worried sigh, she pulled her headset down to rest on her neck and took a sip of water, praying there would only be another few seconds of interference before the horny wayfarer with the offending CB moved out of range.

The voice blared, "Dirty Mama, your ol' Lover Buddy's *ho-ongry.* How about something hot and wet?" Static, followed by an obscene chuckle. Aly blanched. She could only thank Providence they weren't privy to both sides of this off-color conversation. She had a feeling Lover Buddy hadn't been suggesting a bowl of chicken-noodle soup and Dirty Mama's answer would have blistered the paint on the walls.

The audience was tittering with laughter. Aly could only offer a sickly smile as Lover Buddy oozed, "Sweet tha-ang! I'm gonna have me a wreck if you keep talking that way."

Blessed static.

Aly had no idea she'd even looked up until her gaze was snagged by a pair of arresting, cobalt eyes that totally captured her attention.

"You love it and you know it. Come on?" Lover Buddy drawled lecherously. "No man'll ever do ya as hot and sweet as I do. Come back?"

As static filled the air, Aly swallowed, unable to pull her regard from the man in black. He languidly inclined his head, offering her a slow, wicked smile.

Her gazed widened at his unspoken taunt. He was right, she thought. "Dirty Mama" mightn't be able to get better satisfaction than from "ol' Lover Buddy," but Aly knew in her heart that she could go out with all the hardworking types in the world, but she would never know anything equal to Rourk Rountree's caresses. Unfortunately, his heated stare told her he knew it—and *he knew* she knew it. Blast his egotistical hide!

More static gave way to, "Start warmin' them buns, Dirty Mama, I'll be there in—" Static mixed with garbled words.

The CB sizzle finally faded into nothingness. Aly took in a long, shaky breath, not realizing she'd stopped breathing, then gulped down the rest of her water. Replacing her headset, she cleared her throat and apologized weakly. "Don't worry, folks. There'll be no extra charge for that."

The audience snickered as she hurriedly began her chant again, a little more breathily than before. After a minute—half in anticipation and half in dread—her gaze flitted nervously to the back of the grand ball-room.

Rourk was gone.

Disconcerted, she pointedly looked away, hoping no one noticed the unprofessional catch in her voice.

11

ALY WAS DRESSED AND ready for her date with John. She'd been dressed and ready for nearly an hour, and according to her wristwatch, she still had forty-five minutes to wait. Hopping up from her perch on the edge of the bed, she paced her bedroom, too nervous, confused and stressed to sit still.

She'd kept herself busy straightening the ballroom from three—when the last purchaser left with his booty—until after five. By then, there'd been absolutely nothing else to do, so she'd come up to her room, showered and changed. Now it was only six-fifteen. Maude and Merle had taken Jenna to the kitchen to feed her and fix dinner for themselves.

All alone up here on the third floor, Aly was beginning to feel the emptiness of the place close in on her. The incessant pacing came to an abrupt halt when she caught a glimpse of herself in the dresser mirror. It wasn't much of a mirror, for all the really good furniture had been auctioned. These pieces, modestly priced things purchased for use in servants quarters some fifty years ago, were showing both their age and their mediocrity.

Aly had pulled her hair back with combs, but curls grazed her brow and billowed out from the crown of her head. She smiled at herself, testing the expression, then grimaced. She was haggard from lack of sleep and unrelenting tension—most of which had nothing to do with this gargantuan auction she was in charge of. She'd camouflaged the dark smudges beneath her eyes with makeup, and she'd disguised her pallor with the miracle of blush.

Her lipstick had been carefully applied, but somehow her lips seemed too thin. Probably because her anxiety over Rourk kept her so tense her mouth had gone permanently taut with worry. She tested her smile again, noting the lack of happy glisten in her eyes.

Poor John. She only hoped she could hold up her end of the conversational patter tonight. She felt guilty for practically manipulating him into asking her out, so she really owed him a pleasant evening. Unfortunately, all she wanted to do was sprawl on her bed and pound her pillow and wail. She wasn't exactly sure why. She wasn't sure of anything these days. But somehow she seemed to think it would help. Primal wailing, maybe? A woman's version of going to the gym and punching a bag to assuage her frustrations? She didn't know. Maybe all she was doing was mental babbling—*neurotic* mental babbling. Or maybe she was absolutely normal. After all, it had been a long time since she'd had a "date."

She shook her head at herself. "You can handle this, Aly," she muttered. "It's only one lousy date. High-school girls do it all the time! Don't worry so much. Forget about you-know-who. Just go out and have a nice evening."

She gave herself a final, critical glare. The two-piece dress she'd chosen had been referred to in the discount catalog as "a breezy, chic solution for office or socializing." The blouse was a button-shoulder T-shirt and the skirt was a knee-length, pleated dirndl. The synthetic fabric was almost starkly white and didn't do a thing for her pale complexion, but it was the only dress she'd brought with her. Dating hadn't been on her agenda when she'd packed three weeks ago.

With a sigh of discontent, she decided to go down to the kitchen. At least she'd have distracting company while she fidgeted.

Maude was dishing Jenna's dinner onto her sectioned plate and guffawing when Aly entered. Merle was tending something that sizzled on the stove, and Jenna was banging her spoon on her high-chair tray.

"What'd they say?" shouted Merle, turning from her work at the stove.

"It was that Velda woman from Thaddeus Gulch, Texas, again," Maude yelled, setting the plate of strained carrots, beef and blueberry-applesauce dessert in front of Jenna.

Aly settled in the chair beside her daughter and took the baby spoon from her chubby fingers. As she began to feed Jenna, she turned to view the TV, discovering they were watching the home-shopping channel. So, what else was new?

"Oh, hi, Aly," Maude bellowed, dipping behind the nearest refrigerator door as she searched for something. "Remember that Velda woman, who buys stuff almost every hour?"

"Sure," hollered Merle. "Needs therapy."

"She says it *is* therapy," Maude rejoined.

"Whatever. What was so funny?"

"Well," Maude explained, closing the refrigerator door with an elbow, her hands filled with fresh broccoli, "she was telling Tiffany, there, that yesterday two UPS trucks pulled up to her house, and get this! Everything on *both* trucks was for her!"

As Jenna gummed a bite of carrots, Aly grew fascinated by a statuesque blonde on the screen gleefully exuding the attributes of a free-form, pea-green lamp that could be turned on and off by clapping one's hands twice—or by any loud noise that came twice in quick succession. The blonde spoke with such awe and delight, anyone would think the lamp also held the cure for the common cold.

Aly smiled inwardly, envisioning an evening of TV viewing that included any movie starring John Wayne or Clint Eastwood. That lamp would be flashing on and off so much the CIA would probably have the owners investigated on suspicion of sending government secrets by a heinously clever code.

Merle asked loudly, "Everything on both trucks was for Velda?"

Wondering if her ears were playing tricks, Aly turned away from the nightmare of modern light fixtures to face her mother.

Maude was nodding. "Velda said she now had all her Christmas shopping done."

Merle cackled. "Who's she buying Christmas presents for—*France?*"

Despite her dour mood, Aly grinned, saying, "You two are bound and determined to convince me you don't really do all that much TV shopping, aren't you?" She scooped up a spoonful of beef and aimed it toward Jenna's open mouth.

Merle turned the meat she was frying, eyeing her niece for the first time, not appearing to have heard Aly speak. "You look a little tired, dear. Are you feeling all right?"

Aly's teasing grin wavered as Jenna took the bite. "I'm fine," she said, louder. "What are you cooking? Smells good."

"Fried liver, broccoli and Brussels sprouts."

Aly made a sick face. "How could it smell that good? I hate all those things."

Merle made a tsking sound. "We know you don't like them. That's exactly why your mother and I decided to treat ourselves tonight. When we were girls, fried liver, broccoli and Brussels sprouts was our favorite meal."

"You're both twisted," she teased, then more seriously, she said, "But I really appreciate your taking care of Jenna for me tonight."

"We love it," Maude hollered. "We don't get to have her enough without you hoverin'. It'll be a treat for us."

Jenna gurgled, and slapped her hands on the highchair tray, making her plate dance around. Accustomed to Jenna's playful eating habits, Aly dipped into the carrots and deposited another bite in her mouth.

"You look lovely for your date," interjected Maude as she washed the broccoli and dumped it in a pot of water. "That young man, John, is a nice boy. A bit dull, but nice."

"Dull?" Aly objected, wiping dribbling carrots from Jenna's chin with her new Mickey Mouse bib. "I don't think he's dull at all." It wasn't completely the truth, but for some reason she felt she had to defend her date, if for no better reason than the fact that he *was* her date.

"Well," Maude added, depositing the saucepan full of broccoli on the stove, "I just mean whenever he chats with me he always talks about weather or sports."

"Two perfectly respectable subjects. I prefer to think of John as solid," Aly said, aiming more beef Jenna's way. "Besides, I bet even Dwight D. Eisenhower had his dull moments." Aly knew full well what she was doing. The famous Kansas native was purported to be a distant relative on her mother's side of the family—so distant, in fact, that marrying an Eisenhower cousin to a Meeks cousin wouldn't do a speck of damage to their offsprings' gene pool. Still, Maude and Merle were fiercely possessive of their relationship to the former president, and any less-than-sterling comment about wonderful Dwight set them off. That was just fine with Aly. She wanted the subject channeled away from her date.

"Never for one instant was Dwight dull!" Maude insisted. "He was the wittiest president ever to grace the White House. Isn't he the one who said, 'You can lead a horse to water, but you can't make him float?'"

Aly coughed out a startled laugh. "Well, if he didn't, he should have." Her tension easing slightly, she smiled. "I'm sure President Eisenhower was terribly witty, Mother. I was only kidding you."

"I should hope so," huffed Maude.

Jenna let out a strong, gurgly laugh, dipped her fingers into her food and smeared beef all over her face, apparently deciding her mother wasn't feeding her fast enough.

"There, you see," Aly teased. "Jenna laughed. Even she knows I was kidding." From a nearby stack of paper napkins, Aly wiped Jenna's cheeks clean.

Merle snorted. "Neither of you inherited the Meeks sense of humor."

"Want any liver?" Maude bellowed.

As the older woman dished the crusty brown stuff onto a platter, Aly wrinkled her nose. "Now, *you're* kidding." She flicked a look at her watch. Thirty more minutes!

Before she even knew anything was wrong, a blob of blueberry-applesauce splatted on her watch face. A split second later, she felt the whole plate land facedown in her lap. Horror-stricken, she stared at the ugly, sticky mess that used to be her white skirt.

"Oh, Lord!" she moaned. "What am I going to do. I'll never get the carrots and blueberries out of this dress!"

Neither Maude nor Merle were so hard-of-hearing they could miss Aly's distressed cry. For a moment no one in the kitchen moved. Merle stood with a platter of liver frozen a few inches from the tabletop and Maude held a pot lid dangling in midair. All three women were stunned into silence by Jenna's surprise attack. She'd been giggling, but stopped to suck on a finger.

"Oh, Jenna," Aly admonished, peeling the plate away. "You mustn't throw food."

Merle came out of her stupor and thumped the platter down. "I'll take that. You clean yourself up."

"What am I going to do?" Aly mused aloud. "He'll be here in thirty minutes! This is my only dress."

"Uh—"

Maude's single, uttered syllable sounded so ominous Aly's head snapped up.

"What do you mean by 'Uh'?" she asked.

Maude shrugged, covered the boiling broccoli and smiled sheepishly. "Well, I know of one other dress you could wear. I was saving it for your birthday, but—"

"What dress?" Aly asked, dubious yet hopeful. After all, any dress had to be better than this colorfast abstract rendered in a majority of the four basic food groups.

"You'll be mad," Maude warned.

Aly plucked at the fabric, pulling the wet goo away from her slip. "Mother, I won't be mad. If you have a dress, I'll wear it. I don't have any choice."

"I'll go with you and get it," Maude offered. "Merle, watch the veggies."

Back in Aly's room, she put the skirt to soak in a stain remover her mother had bought via a TV ad. Still, she didn't hold out much hope. She'd never gotten strained carrots or blueberry out of anything yet.

Maude came back in, humming off-key and tearing open a package. When the paper and box were discarded on the bed, Aly was mortified to see that thigh-length, black spandex dress her mother was supposed to have returned to the home-shopping channel. Aly groaned. "Oh, Mother! How *could* you, after I specifically—"

"Hush, now, and put it on," Maude cut in loudly. "You'll look very 'with it.'"

The dress was thrust into her hands, and Aly knew she didn't have any choice but to put it on. Slipping it over her head, she squirmed and wiggled as her mother tugged down. Finally, after a struggle, it settled into place.

Merle beamed. "There, you see. You look just like that model, Mojo or something. You have such long pretty legs."

"Bare white legs," Aly mumbled. "And practically all showing."

"Here," Maude said, rummaging in the box. "Black hose. Perfect. You already have black shoes."

"My flats I wear at auctions—"

"You're all set!" Maude plunked her fists on her hips and smiled the smile of a proud mother. "You're gorgeous. Now finish getting ready. My liver's getting cold." Kissing her daughter fondly on the cheek, she shouted, "Have a good time, tonight. Oh, and on your way out, if you see Rourk, tell him dinner's ready." She turned to go, yelling, "Haven't seen hide nor hair of that young man all day."

I have, Aly mused in silent frustration as she nodded toward her mother's receding back. The memory of him standing in the grand ballroom's entrance, staring at her with that "You love me and you know it" expression—so haunting, so damnably sure of himself— still frazzled her nerves when she chanced to recall it. And unfortunately for her, that scenario replayed itself before her mind's eye every few minutes, no matter how hard she tried to block it from her thoughts.

Dropping dejectedly to the bed, Aly toyed with the cellophane wrapper that encased the hosiery. Unhappy, she scanned herself. Actually, the dress fit as though it had been made for her. The neck was scooped, but it wasn't indecent. More creamy breast showed than she was used to, though certainly not more than a moderate society allowed. And she liked dresses with cap sleeves. There was nothing lewd about cap sleeves. The back plunged a bit, but, still it wasn't anything she'd get arrested for.

All too aware that she had no other options at this point, she ripped into the hosiery wrapping and slithered into the panty hose. Stepping into her flats, she grabbed up her only purse, which, luckily, happened to be black.

Scanning herself in the mirror, she could do no more than gape, her brow creased in worry. She hadn't planned on looking quite so—so sultry. Actually, her plan had been to look *clean*. If she didn't know better, she'd think the woman in the mirror was out to snag a man tonight. She had a sinking feeling John would think that, too.

An idea struck her. A coat! She dashed to her closet, then lurched to a halt. *For Pete's sake, Aly,* she berated herself. *It's August and ninety degrees outside! You ninny, you didn't bring a coat!*

With a despondent sigh, she peered at the time again. Fifteen minutes left. All her nervous tension came flooding back, tenfold. Maybe a calming walk in the garden would help.

The evening air was warm and still. Though there was over an hour of daylight left, the patio lay in shadow, for the sun had slipped behind the roof's western peak. With its covering of decorative trees, the garden area was darkened further, giving it a dusky, storybook tranquillity. Soft scents beckoned, giving the flower-filled haven a charmed, romantic aura.

As Aly drifted from the patio along the stone path, she decided that some sensitive landscape architect had visualized this place years ago as a Shangri-la of muted sights and restful sounds. A sanctuary for the heart, mind and soul. She silently thanked his foresight, for she loved this quiet refuge, and even a brief visit here never failed to compose her.

Reaching out, Aly trailed her finger along the bud of an exquisite silver rose, turned to dark Wedgwood blue in the prenumbral evening. She smiled, almost able to forget her problems for the moment. This must be what was meant by the old cliché, "Stop to smell the roses." Nature's serene wonders held a more calming effect for her than any man-made tranquilizer could even attempt.

She rounded the bench and sat down. Within the cocoon of darkness, she was practically invisible, all in black, which was just fine with her. If only she and John could spend their date here. He might never know she had on anything more revealing than a flour sack.

She sank back against the gnarled redbud and closed her eyes. When she opened them again it was because she thought she'd heard a noise. She was confronted by a lanky pair of legs, black loafers and bare ankles. Wearing black, Rourk, too, was all but invisible in the shadows. She lifted her startled gaze to his face. His expression was pleasant but not overtly so. She might as well have been a stranger sharing a bus stop.

"Hi," he murmured quietly. "Small world."

Quickly pulling herself together, she crossed her arms before her, hoping to appear relaxed. "Dinner—" She cleared the squeak from her voice and went on, "Dinner's ready."

He looked away, staring off across the pond. "I'm sure it is."

"It's liver, broccoli and Brussels sprouts," she babbled, wanting him to leave her to herself for a few peaceful minutes, though she feared her attempts at calm, now, would be futile.

He chuckled. "Sounds delicious." Still presenting her with his profile, he added, "I think I'll pass."

He was standing there looking all too casual and relaxed, hands in his pockets, clearly planning to settle in for the evening. Aly exhaled a defeated sigh, saying, "I suppose you want to sit in your garden, so I'll go."

"Stay," he commanded softly. "I've been wondering how it went today."

She was surprised that he was finally showing any interest in how much money the auction had made. Most owners would be chomping at the bit to know everything down to the last decimal point the instant it was over. Rourk had seemed not only disinterested, but almost contemptuous of the whole process. Or perhaps he was only disinterested and contemptuous of her.

She pretended to study a red-leafed shrub, almost black in the darkness, explaining, "You made something over six-hundred thousand."

Silence reigned.

Finally, unable to stand the suspense, she had to chance a peek at his profile. She needed to know if he was bored, pleased or if he'd had a heart attack from the excitement. When she peered up at him, he was watching her, his expression solemn. She felt the warmth drain from her face at his relentless scrutiny. "What?" she whispered, her voice hovering on the verge of extinction.

He gave her an enigmatic shrug. "So, what movie are you and John going to see?"

She was taken aback by the abrupt subject change and asked, "Didn't you hear me? I said you made over six hundred *thousand* dollars today."

"I'll make several million tomorrow," he reminded. "Next weekend I'll make millions more. I think we've already established I'm a millionaire, Aly." He raised a questioning brow. "So, what movie are you and John going to see?"

"Something with Jeff Bridges," she mumbled, not sure why she was even bothering to talk to him.

"I've heard it's good," he said. "But sad."

She was uncomfortable exchanging meaningless small talk with him. They'd shared so much passionate intimacy, they should forever be beyond the sort of conversation you'd have with a stranger on a plane. She couldn't figure out his game. "I like sad movies," she retorted. It came out sounding defensive.

Sliding his hands from his pockets, he indicated the bench. "Mind if I sit?"

"It's your house, but—" she eyed him begrudgingly "—I came out here to be alone, actually."

"So did I." He tossed her a wry half grin. "But here we are." He inclined his head and said, "I'll just sit. I won't bite."

She had a mind to tell him she knew better than that, recalling his sexy nipping along her breasts and inner thighs, but the mere thought brought back such hot memories, she couldn't find words. Suddenly trembly, she rasped, "Go ahead."

"Nice evening," he commented, once he'd settled a few inches from her on the cement lawn-seat.

"For August."

He chuckled again.

Irked by his good mood, she asked a little more brusquely than she meant to, "What's so funny?"

He faced her, murmuring, "Us." His eyes seemed depthless, jet-black and much too sensual in the darkness. "We're funny, Aly," he was saying. "I love you and you love me, yet we're sitting here in strained conversation as though we're not sure where we've seen each other before. That's funny, don't you think?"

She looked away, too cowardly to meet his probing stare. His admission seared her core but she vowed not to show it. When she could trust her voice, she muttered, "Hysterical."

"It's just as much my fault as yours," he conceded.

She jerked around to glare at him. "How magnanimous of you to admit, considering I ran from *you* at every turn."

There was a brief, incredulous twitch of his brows. It wasn't much, but it was enough to remind her who snatched whose towel from whose naked body. She swallowed and flicked her glance as far away as possible.

"What I meant, was," he began again, "I've been doing a lot of thinking since the other night. And I've discovered something pretty disgusting about myself."

She stared purposefully into the distance, not speaking for a long time. Finally, when he said nothing more, she gave up and exhaled distractedly. *"What?"* She cautiously faced him, frowning, angry with herself for being drawn into this conversation at all. "What did you discover that was so disgusting?"

He stretched his legs before him. The movement drew Aly's gaze. Even in the low light, she could make out the flexing and bunching of his solid thighs. Appalled with herself, she cast her glance down to her own lap.

"I'm still a controlling bastard," he said.

She started at the unexpected admission, staring sharply in his direction.

He surveyed her, his lips twisting ruefully. "Old habits die hard, Aly. I love you and I want you, but I realize now, I'm still demanding things on my own terms."

She gaped, nonplused.

"I'm sorry for getting on your case about being a control freak," he added softly. "It's not my business."

"Are you serious?" she demanded in a rough whisper.

He turned away. His square jaw tensed for a moment before he said, "I'm quite serious."

Rourk's classically handsome profile was strong and rigid at this moment, very solemn. She squinted into the darkness, straining to watch him closely. After a long stretch of time, she said, "So what are you saying? You're going to leave me alone?"

"Is that what you want?" he asked gravely, as though he already knew the answer.

"Yes," she breathed, not convinced she meant it. Of course, this was for the best, but her heart was thumping painfully at the idea of never feeling his mouth against hers again, or knowing the erotic delight of his fingers along her naked hip.

He nodded, and even in the vague light, she sensed his expression had become distant, his manner withdrawn.

"You give up easily," she stated, her tone going tart. "But I suppose that goes with the territory."

He smiled then—an odd, satiric smile—but still he didn't face her. "Maybe you're right. Maybe I'll spend the rest of my life giving up easily. Maybe I'm not much of a man." He shook his head. "I hope that's not true. To be honest, I'm not sure what I am or who I am. I've been somebody else all my life—for my father." The last word came out sharp and bitter. Stopping to regain control, he ran a distracted hand through his hair, then continued more quietly, "Right now I need to quit trying to control other people and look for the person I really am. Fix myself. I hope I turn out to be somebody better than the man I've been in the past."

"Or the present?" Aly blurted, then bit her lip. That was unnecessarily cruel. Her only excuse was that she was torn up inside, but for all the wrong reasons. She felt terribly rejected—ironically so, for she didn't even want a relationship with this man! Why was she hurting so much, then? Rourk was doing exactly what she'd demanded of him, time and time again: *leaving her alone*.

He shifted to glance her way, then stood. There was a new air of isolation about him as though he were pushing her away from him emotionally. His faint smile held a touch of sadness. "Seeing myself in the mirror of your eyes has been a rude awakening for me, Aly. I only wish I could help you in some way—to find your own peace."

She knew he meant to be kind. What a paradox that her dislike for him had somehow helped him begin a turnaround. But to what? And when? She shrugged, mumbling, "You don't owe me anything, Rourk. Please . . . Let's just forget—everything. . . ."

"I can't do that," he said. "I still love you. That hasn't changed."

She clamped her fists together. *And I still love you!* her mind cried. But she refused to admit it. What purpose would it serve? Instead she offered feebly, "Nobody's perfect, Rourk. Not you, not me. We'll survive."

"Survival is enough for you?" he challenged, drawing her gaze.

She flinched at his reprimand, then frowned. "You're doing it again. I thought you said you were through controlling other people."

He made a guttural sound—not quite a chuckle, more an apologetic grunt. "As I said, old habits die hard. Forgive me."

She nodded, lowering her head in abashment.

A few seconds later, she felt a hand on her arm, helping her up as Rourk coaxed, "It's seven."

She was too startled by the gallantry to pull away. Avoiding his face, she mumbled, "Oh—better go."

She moved without conscious thought toward the glass double doors, numb inside, her wits too muddled to make sense out of what had just happened. He loved her, but he knew she didn't want anything to do with him, so he was leaving her alone? She could be a control freak day and night, night and day, for the rest of her life? She could go out with John or—or even Elmer Fudd if she chose? No more Mr. Slovenly-Domineering-Critical on her case—or on her, uh—

It startled her when the patio door was opened for her. Unwittingly, she pivoted to face Rourk and was shocked at his savage expression. With the lessening of the shade on the patio, they could see each other clearly, and it was apparent that Rourk, at least, didn't like what he saw.

His eyes ranged over her, dark emotion marring his face. "Damn. Is that what you intend to wear tonight?" he ground out.

She stiffened. "I thought you were getting off my case!"

They stared at each other across a sizzling silence. His glare burned through her, but after a moment the corners of his mouth twisted in wry exasperation. "Hell, Aly," he growled. "It's just that I don't relish sending the woman I love out on dates, especially dressed to—"

"You don't have to stay, you know," she shot back, hurting inside. Hurting for him and—Lord help her foolishness—hurting for her. She loved him, no matter how bad he was for her, and she couldn't help herself.

Rourk's nostrils flared, revealing his jealousy and pain, but he merely nodded, his face becoming a pleasant mask. "You're right." Stepping back to allow her through, he muttered thickly, "Have a nice time."

She whirled away and stomped through the patio doors, her common sense insisting she should feel *free, happy, unencumbered!*

She did, she told herself. Absolutely.

The door slammed shut at her back, but just before the loud bang, and the telltale tinkle of broken glass, she heard a muffled blasphemy. Rourk was as angry as hell. She wondered if he was more angry at her or at himself.

The doorbell was chiming grandly and she ran to open it, trying to push the unruly softness she harbored for the master of the mansion from her brain. It was a stupid softness that she couldn't afford.

John, exactly on time, stood there, all cleaned and scrubbed and grinning, wearing a dark blue suit, white shirt and blue-and-red-striped tie. "Well," she enthused with a wide smile, "don't you look great!"

Grasping him by the arm, she hurried him down the wide steps as though the devil himself were chasing her, firmly resolving to have a perfect evening.

As John turned away to fumble in his pocket for the car keys, Aly unobtrusively wiped away a foolish tear.

12

THE NEXT MORNING, ALY was up early baking a huge coffee cake for her crew while she tried to get Jenna fed. By seven-thirty, the cinnamon-bread aroma wafted all through the first floor of the mansion, so when she opened the door to Mark, John, Dave and George, they all enthused, "Smells good! I'm starved," in comic unison.

As Aly was closing the door, the two off-duty police officers she'd hired as security drove up in Brodie Brown's car. Aly had used Brodie before, but the other one—Hal Goode—was a friend of Brodie's, and was new to Aly. She was a bit startled when this other police officer stepped out of the passenger seat, and a long expanse of feminine leg appeared.

Brodie, a lanky forty-year-old father of five, waved. His balding pate reflected the morning sun. "Hi, Aly," he boomed. "Meet Officer Goode."

As the two cops came up the steps, Aly was struck by how pretty Officer Goode was. Quite tall, probably five feet ten, she had the most striking cap of red curls Aly had ever seen. And she was wearing a savvy navy suit that accentuated her trim, leggy figure. Upon closer inspection, Aly noticed that the woman had intelligent green eyes and a pleasantly angular, frecklestrewn face.

Aly stuck out a hand, "Hi, Officer Goode, I'm Aly Fields. Thanks for giving up your Sunday to do security for us. As soon as my mother and aunt get here from the lawyer's safe, we'll have a lot of valuable jewelry on the premises. We've never had any trouble, but having two armed officers on duty makes me feel better."

The redhead shook Aly's hand and grinned, "Happy to do it. I'm a single mom and the money helps." As they headed up the steps she added, "But call me Hal. It's short for Halcyone. Nobody calls me that, though."

"Not if they want to live," Brodie said with a chuckle, as he loped along beside them. "She's a damn fine shot, and she shoots to kill. Right, Hal?"

Hal laughed out loud; the sound was husky and rich. "Don't exaggerate, Brodie. I've only put a couple of people in Intensive Care."

"I've heard that about you hot redheads."

Aly grinned at their kidding, then said, "Want some coffee cake? You can meet the other folks who'll be working today."

When they entered the kitchen, Aly was baffled by how quiet it got. All four males glanced up from their devoted attention to cutting coffee cake and pouring coffee to stare at the attractive female addition.

Aly broke the silence with, "You guys know Brodie. This is his new partner, Officer Hal Goode. She'll be helping us cover security today."

Everybody spoke at once, offering Hal a chair, a cup of coffee or thrusting her a plate of cake. As Aly resumed feeding Jenna, she quietly observed the hubbub at the table as her crew and her security force chatted. What most surprised her—but pleasantly so—were the sparks of attraction that seemed to be flying between Hal and John. Instant rapport.

As Hal exuded her disbelief that John was *also* going to run in the ten-mile Wichita Turkey Trot on Thanksgiving Day, Aly rested her chin in her hands and simply watched. John was suggesting that Hal and he train together.

Aly smiled. She was glad about this unexpected turn of events. She'd had a terrible time last night on their date. She and John had both tried, but they'd discovered soon enough that nothing romantic would come of it. When he'd dropped her off, he hadn't even tried to kiss her good-night. There hadn't been anything uncomfortable about it; oddly enough, they'd simply realized they were meant to be nothing more than co-workers and friends. That was enough.

"I'll pick you up at six tomorrow morning," John was saying. "School starts at nine."

Hal smiled and took a notebook from her purse, where Aly could see the glint of gunmetal. "Let me give you my address," she said, writing and then passing him a page.

Jenna banged the flats of both palms on her tray and pulled Aly's attention back to what she was supposed to be doing. Still, it gave Aly a nice feeling, knowing John and Hal had found each other because of their association with her.

Maude and Merle could be heard coming long before they entered the kitchen with a big metal lockbox. "Whew, this stuff weights a ton. Who's gonna help us set up?"

"I'd better go," Hal said to John, with a slight brush of his hand.

"I'll be right in. Can't wait to meet your little girl," he said.

Hal smiled. "We'll fix you dinner one night soon."

John beamed his pleasure at the idea as the red-headed officer left the kitchen with Maude, Merle and George.

"When are you two going to eat?" Aly shouted after her mother and aunt.

"When are you gonna help?" Maude yelled back.

With a laugh, Aly shook her head and said, "Okay, Jenna. Looks like the workday's begun."

Time passed, and people started to arrive. Aly's eyes kept shifting to the ballroom entrance every time anyone new walked in. She checked her watch. Almost nine. The jewelry auction would begin soon, and Rourk hadn't come down, not even for breakfast.

Maude sat at a table by the door, registering individuals and giving out bidder numbers. Over five hundred people were there, previewing the jewelry or standing in little clusters chatting like family at a reunion, for that's what the auction circuit was for many regulars—like family reunions.

Everybody knew everybody. Aly spotted "The Corn Lady." She was an eighty-seven-year-old Kansas farm woman, one of the delightful eccentrics who'd been attending Bean auctions ever since Aly could remember. The Corn Lady was called that because when she first started collecting, all she had to trade was corn. After more than sixty years of collecting, she'd amassed one of the finest hoards of antique jewelry in the country.

She flapped a beringed hand at Aly and toddled on her way. Clad all in black, she sported a black felt Western hat with a diamond-studded band. Beneath its broad brim, a thick, gray braid dangled over her left shoulder to well past her waist. As always, she had on a black silk fringed shirt, ankle-length black denim skirt and high-heeled boots. Her scrawny neck glistened with weighty gems and her spindly arms were cuffed nearly to the elbows with diamonds, pearls and other costly stones.

"Aly," she croaked, with an elfish smile, "that precious baby has grown so. And two more teeth."

Aly was used to this. Regulars felt like kin, and the Corn Lady was practically a great-grandmother to Jenna. She'd given her a prized pair of tiny diamond earrings when she was born. "Miss Aggie," Aly teased, "I'll give Jenna to you any time you say. She's getting another tooth, and she's as cranky as you were last month when you were outbid on that pair of chandelier ear—"

"*Oh!*" Aggie groaned with a curt wave of her knobby hand. "Don't remind me of those earrings! That Priscilla Hogg distracted me with a wild story about that crazy niece and her travelling salesman *ex*-fiancé, and I— Well, I can't abide talking about it, but Priscilla's on my bad list. I won't be sitting next to that gossip today, I tell you!"

"I saw Priscilla earlier. She swore that engagement's back on." Aly looked at her watch. "It's nine. Maybe you should be getting a good seat."

The Corn Lady fiddled with her bracelets, trying to uncover a bejeweled watch, apparently needing to verify the time herself. "Mercy me. I haven't even checked out that diamond-and-topaz peacock brooch. Excuse me, honey—"

Aggie-the-Corn-Lady tottered off with her quick, tiny steps, and Aly shook her head after her. The hunched-over woman was so frail she could hardly walk, but she insisted on wearing those precarious, high-heeled cowboy boots. Turning away with a sigh, Aly had to smile. Sweet eccentrics like The Corn Lady made the world a more interesting place. They certainly added richness and fun to the often-tedious auction business.

Someone tall and dark entered the ballroom door, and Aly's gaze was drawn there, her heartbeat growing more rapid in anticipation. But just as quickly, her excitement ebbed. It was only Ed Cathgate, a jewelry dealer from Chicago. Trying not to care if Rourk ever showed his face again, she gave Ed a friendly wave and headed toward the podium. It was time to start the auction.

At three-thirty that afternoon, everyone was gone, including John, who'd given Hal a ride home. Brodie stood by, insisting on remaining as Aly counted up the day's balance. Four million dollars and some change. *Four million!* And Rourk hadn't even deigned to leave his room. Well, if that was the way Mr. I-Don't-Give-A-Damn felt about his inheritance, that was just fine with her.

"He's gone!" Merle bellowed, huffing into the grand ballroom where Maude and Aly were stacking money and checks.

Aly looked up, confused, "Who, Aunt Merle?"

"Rourk. He's gone." She thrust out a hand. There was a white, letter-size envelope in it. "This is for you, Aly. Found it on his bed."

Aly looked at the letter her aunt held, unable, for some reason, to reach out and take it. She could only stare as a feeling of foreboding flooded through her. Rourk was gone, and she knew why before even reading the message.

Merle walked over to the table and thrust it in Aly's face. "Well, aren't you curious?" she shouted.

Aly took it tentatively, as though it were a telegram from the War Department. *Someone you love is gone forever.* That's what it said, she was sure. But it couldn't be helped. The man she loved wasn't good for her. He didn't like her the way she was and spent all his time trying to change her. That was no basis for a relationship. She couldn't change, didn't want to. She wasn't a control freak. She was just a single mother with lots of responsibilities and pressures.

Aly tore open the envelope. The letter tumbled out onto a pile of one-hundred-dollar bills, toppling it.

"What's it say?" demanded Merle, snatching it up before Aly had time to read it.

"Let's see," Merle mumbled, scanning it, then frowning. "Says he doesn't want to be here to send you off on your dates. Says he's—"

"Give her that!" Maude rebuked, yanking the page from her sister. "Merle, you were always such a snoop. Why, the ink was never even dry on my diary before you had your big honker in there reading all my secrets."

"Secrets!" Merle shot back. "You call that silly-little-girl foolishness you wrote about 'secrets'! Why, fantasies is what they were. Pure . . ."

Aly's mind drifted away from her aunt's bellowed diatribe as she read Rourk's bold handwriting.

Dear Aly,
Don't expect me to stand around seeing you off on your dates. Once was enough.

I suppose it's time I started to fix myself. It had to come, sooner or later. Too bad for both of us it wasn't—before the towel.

Be happy,
Rourk

Aly crumpled the sheet of paper. So he was gone. Gone. Suddenly that was a big, empty, lonely word. Gone to "fix" himself—whatever that was supposed to mean. She swallowed the bile that had risen in her throat. That was the way with men like him. Lazy, self-centered vagabonds. When things got too intense, they just went somewhere else to wreak their havoc on new, unsuspecting women. Well, well— *Good riddance*, her mind cried, but her heart was weighted down with despair.

Abruptly she vaulted up, determined not to let his quick departure upset her. Fumbling with the fallen bills, she began to stack and gather them for transport to the Rountree lawyer's safe.

There must have been something about her hasty activity that was out of character, for both Maude and Merle grew suddenly quiet, halting their shouted harangue and turning toward her in unspoken unison.

"What's wrong, Aly?" Maude asked, her tone shrill but concerned. "You look sick. Did he say something that made you unhappy?"

"I had it almost read," Merle shot back, offended. "It was about dates and a trowel, or towel, I think."

"Oh, hush up, Nosy Nellie," Maude hollered. "Let Aly talk."

Aly shook her head, piling the bills into the metal box they'd brought the jewels in that morning. "He just said he had to go. Nothing important."

"Fix towels, or something," Merle added helpfully.

"Fix *towels?*" Maude snapped with a dubious frown. "That speed-reading course you took in '69 was a big waste! What would a man like that be doing *fixing towels*. He's no terry-cloth repair person!"

"Well, he—"

"Brodie, we'd better get going," Aly cut in loudly, if a little unsteadily. "We need to get this money in the lawyer's safe."

As Brodie took the heavy case from her trembly fingers, she struggled hard to appear nonchalant, even though her emotions were in turmoil. *Oh, why can't I erase Rourk Rountree's image from my heart as easily as he could pack up and leave?*

LABOR DAY WEEKEND WOULD be a big one for Bean Auction. The biggest yet, probably. The Rountree grand ballroom would be packed, for the extra holiday gave faraway buyers more travel time. Aly was looking forward to it like a medieval peasant looked forward to the Black Plague. Her heart simply wasn't in it.

Rourk had been gone since Sunday. It was Friday, and the preview of Mrs. Rountree's eclectic batch of collections would begin in an hour. Aly sat before her mirror, staring at her gaunt image, recalling what Merle had told her last night after she'd come back from running an errand in downtown Wichita. She'd barged into Aly's room after ten o'clock, shouting, "I saw Rourk!"

Jenna had been fretful and unable to sleep, so Aly was rubbing a teething medication on her daughter's gums. With her aunt's unexpected intrusion, she'd almost tossed both the medicine bottle and her baby into the air, she'd been so startled. Gathering her wits, she'd cried, "For heaven's sake, Aunt Merle, you scared the life out of me."

To add to the strain and chaos of the moment, Jenna began to bawl loudly.

"He was having dinner with a very attractive lady in that new fancy restaurant on Main," Merle explained.

"You know, the one that's inside that fancy new hotel?"

Aly tried not to care that he was already casting his sexy spell over another woman—in a restaurant connected to a hotel, yet! "It's none of our business," she murmured, and then, realizing her aunt hadn't heard that, said more loudly, "I thought you were just dropping off a few letters in the postbox."

"Was," Merle nodded defiantly. "But when I passed by that bright red Porsche convertible in the hotel parking lot, I turned in out of curiosity. Don't see many bright red Porsches with a tag that reads, Wings-1, even though Wichita is 'The Air Capital of the World.' So, I decided to go in and say hello."

Aly closed her eyes for a brief moment, not allowing herself to speak, for fear she'd say something she'd regret.

"He said to tell you hello, too," Merle went on, blithely unaware of Aly's torment.

Aly nodded, gritting sarcastically, "That's swell." Funny, somehow, she didn't think he'd be that type. She'd thought he'd changed—been sincere when he'd told her he cared. Maybe the pretty woman was his therapist. She almost laughed at that. Talk about grasping at straws!

She supposed the fact that she was surprised Merle had seen him out with a woman told her something of her insight—at least where one sexy smooth-talker was concerned. She was far from perfect at gauging people, that was for sure. With a barely audible moan, she jumped up, patting her squalling baby. She'd spent more than a healthy chunk of her waking hours fretting about Rourk. It was high time she moved on. Gathering her courage about her like a cloak, she faced her aunt. "I'd better get Jenna settled in bed," she shouted over the shrieking. "Good night, Aunt Merle."

Her aunt scurried away after that, oblivious of the fact that she'd ruined any chance of sleep for her niece that night. And now, as Aly stared at her bleak reflection, she could no longer force back the nettling question from her mind: Who was this "pretty woman" Rourk had been wining and dining last night? It was painfully clear that he was every bit as casual with his "I love you" speeches as he was about everything else that touched his life.

Something sparkled before her, drawing her attention, and her stomach twisted at what she saw. A tear—a lousy, stupid, foolish tear—trembling on her lower lashes. For some reason, witnessing her own despair over this unsuitable man was finally too much, and she buried her face in her hands and sobbed.

Why hadn't he been able to understand? She *had* to be in control! So many people depended on her—her mother, her aunt, her daughter. There were the bills Jack had left behind for her to make right—and even sweet *George* counted on her! So many people needed her to be strong. She *wasn't* a control freak, just an everyday single mother with responsibilities. That's why she fought so hard for mastery over a natural desire to be taken care of, to curl up in some strong man's lap and be petted and loved. She'd learned the hard way that that sort of paradise was a total myth! So, as long as she was in charge, nobody could use her, or hurt her again—or any of her family.

Consumed with stress and feeling lost and weary, she dropped her head to the crook of her elbow and sobbed. She cried for herself, her weaknesses, her vow never to make the same mistakes again—and for the tragic fact that she had made them again. She cried because she loved a man who'd professed to love her, but didn't like her the way she was, and now, apparently was well over the grieving process of losing her. Struck by the irony, she found herself laughing bitterly amid her broken sobs. It was a forlorn, frightening sound, like the laugh of a woman driven mad by grief amid a roomful of weeping mourners.

A loud knock sounded at her door. "Aly, can I borrow your iron?" her mother shouted through the door. "My black skirt fell off its hanger and it's a real mess."

Aly swiped harshly at her eyes and took in several shuddery breaths. "Sure," she called, working to regain her composure. "I'll—I'll bring it in to you in a minute. I'm not quite dressed," she lied.

Trying to pull herself together, she moved leadenly into the connecting bathroom and threw cold water on her face. With a stern glance in the mirror over the sink, she warned, "Forget him, Aly. Get on with your life. Find a man with a backbone!" She swallowed hard, murmuring sadly, "There must be a man in the world like that I can love as passionately as—"

Biting off the telling remark, she grabbed the steam iron from a shelf in her closet and fled both her room and her wretched thoughts.

THE AUCTION WAS HALF OVER and the five-minute recess was slipping by with breakneck speed. Aly took a sip of her water and resumed her place at the podium as Mark positioned a heart-shaped condom tin on the turntable. Aly sighed. This was her least-favorite collection. Why it embarrassed her, she didn't know. Maybe it was just the memory of Rourk's off-color comments about his ancestors being such Don Juans in the love department, they'd actually used all these condoms!

Her mind flashed back to the nights she'd spend with him—the hot sex, the gentle, wordless communion—and she felt her skin go fiery.

"What's the matter with you?" shouted Merle, who was standing beside her. "You're red as a ripe tomato."

Aly took another sip of her water from a less-than-steady hand, and shook her head. "Think we should start?" she queried loudly, more to change the subject than to get an approval.

Merle scanned the crowd, her brow creasing in thought. "Looks like they're all getting settled. Might as well."

Aly lifted her wireless mike from her shoulders and called for quiet as she situated the headpiece so that the tiny microphone was located near her mouth. Reminding the audience that item number 405 was now up for auction, she started the bid at fifty dollars.

George stepped up on the opposite side of the turntable and began to move in concert with Aly as the offers came fast and furious. She chanted, motioned, chanted, pointed, gestured in invitation to raise the bid. The heart-shaped tin box was now up to one hundred and forty dollars. Aly's brain shifted into autopilot, her consciousness sliding to thoughts of Rourk. She hated the fact that he still insinuated himself into her mind, into her dreams; hated the fact that he was off again, on another self-indulgent romp, and hated herself that her heart had gone with him—

Booming out over the loudspeaker came the unexpected question, "What if I had a job? Could you love me, then?"

Aly faltered, her gaze darting around. It was happening again. Outside interference on their sound system. But that voice . . .

"I—I'm sorry, folks," Aly apologized tightly, disoriented. "We're having some transmission problems. If you'll—"

"What if I bought a station wagon and wore socks?" the same voice asked, his tone coaxing, deep and very familiar.

Aly searched the room. She was mystified. It couldn't be Rourk's voice!

"It's *Rourk!*" Merle squealed deafeningly, answering her question. "*It's Rourk on the loudspeaker!*" Spinning to grasp Aly by the shoulders, she yelled, "What's he talking about?"

Aly bit her lip, befuddled.

"I love you, Aly. Marry me," came the man's voice, again.

"Oh, my . . ." Aly's words carried through the audience, and the sound of it shocked even her, for she hadn't realized she'd spoken aloud.

"He's proposing!" Maude bellowed, leaping up from the table near the ballroom entrance. "Rourk's proposing marriage. To *Aly!*"

Looking around, the audience began to titter and shift. One man shouted, "Way to go, Aly!"

The Corn Lady stood and waved, crying in her wispy little voice, "How romantic! Is he terribly handsome, Aly? I must meet this boy!"

Aly held up her hands for quiet, but before she could speak, the voice interrupted softly, "I've done a lot of stupid things in my life, but letting you slip through my fingers is not going to be one of them."

She felt a shiver of delight, but squelched it. What about his need to change her? What about that "pretty woman" he was out with just last night? She steeled herself against softening toward him and tried to begin her chant again. Before she could utter a word, she was interrupted again with, "Aly, I'm out front. Come talk to me."

Priscilla Hogg trumpeted, "Go tell him you'll marry him, hon, or I will. Men in socks turn me on!"

"Oh, shut up, Priscilla!" some elderly woman shouted. "Any man not wearing a Rest In Peace slab on his chest turns you on!"

The bidders snickered among themselves. George stared at Aly, his expression closed in confusion. Aly didn't blame him. She was more than a little confused herself. When her glance veered to Mark and John, they smiled broadly as the omnipresent voice cut in with, "Did I ever tell you Jenna called me Dada . . ."

Her face flaming, Aly mumbled into her mike, calling for a break in the bidding. She had to put an end to this craziness. What was wrong with Rourk? He couldn't mean this. They were simply too far apart in their thinking. Against her will, the memory of him being out with a pretty woman flashed in her mind, and jealousy made her blood boil.

She came to a decision. Tearing off her mike, she slammed it on the podium and stalked toward the exit. She'd tell Mr. I-Love-You-When-It-Suits-Me a thing or two and straighten him out once and for all! With every eye glued to her, she marched out of the ballroom and threw open the mansion's double doors, ready for a fierce confrontation.

A cherry-red Porsche was parked at the bottom of the wide band of entry steps. Rourk, so lean, so devastating in his masculine appeal, was leaning indolently against the hood, a cellular phone in his hand.

He flicked his gaze her way, his eyes a pure, deep blue, were unwavering and earnest.

Aly was staggered by his appearance. She remembered him as wonderfully handsome, but somehow, seeing him here like this, was a blow to her heart. An offhandedly elegant man, yet a rugged individualist, he was clad in a slouchy calavera camp shirt, silk-screened in a subtle Native American pattern of sand and bronze on white. Aly noted against her will how the striking design enhanced the breadth of his shoulders and showed to perfection the narrowness of his waist. His hair had been trimmed, and his craggy face was clean-shaven.

She bit the inside of her cheek, unhappy at the dangerous turn of her emotions. His bone-colored slacks fit all too well, hiding none of his natural attributes, but were stylishly drapy, their meticulous pleats gently tapering to crossed ankles. On his feet were rust-colored keltie slip-ons. And—her eyes widened in amazement—did she see socks?

He stood and faced her, his eyes holding her lovingly, their message so soft that some of the sting evaporated from Aly's planned scolding. Her heart was melting fast, her resolve dissolving. Stalling, unsure of herself, on the top step, she forced a hoarse demand through stiffened lips. "What do you think you're doing with that phone?" she cried faintly.

In his eyes a strange sadness rose, a haunted look. "I was proposing. Couldn't you tell?" He held out a hand in invitation. "Come here to me."

She couldn't move, couldn't trust her hearing. She must be hallucinating. Must have had a bad cup of coffee. This couldn't be happening.

After a moment of silence, Rourk's troubled expression gave way to a look of gravity, of yearning. "Aly, please . . ." he coaxed softly. "Come here."

His demeanor was tender, loving, irresistible, and Aly found herself moving toward him in a dreamlike state. When she grew near, she was astonished to see his eyes shimmering with emotion. The sight so unnerved her she couldn't breathe, couldn't speak, could only stare in awe. The man that cared about nothing was near tears.

He half smiled, but it wasn't a merry smile. He took her fingers in his. The heat of his touch brought her back to her senses enough to realize he'd placed his phone on the car's hood. Feeling the intensity of his perusal, she searched his darkly handsome face, his glimmering eyes, his tentative smile. Neither of them talked for a long time. His unwavering scrutiny frightened her—badly frustrating her vow to put him from her heart—but also sent a quiver of happiness cascading through her.

After a taut moment, he urged. "Marry me, Aly."

She stiffened, her practical side rising to do battle. "I—I can't believe you're asking me. I'm a control freak. You don't want—"

He tugged her into his arms, taking possession of her lips, demanding, gentle and knowing. Her thoughts grew jumbled, her resolution blunted. She reeled with delight and a feeling of coming home, instinctively hugging him to her. She relished his solid strength, his scent, the depth of his ardor. But she fought it, though her will was draining away. With a sad moan, she pressed against him, crying, "No . . . no. You said—"

"I know, and I was wrong," he acknowledged, his tone husky and somber. Holding her slightly away from him so that he could stare into her eyes, he admitted, "I was wrong, sweetheart. You're not a control freak. You're just scared and want stability and security in your life." He kissed her briefly, murmuring against her lips, "What you don't understand is that you don't have to do it alone."

He kissed her again, lightly, then lifted his head to gauge her reaction. She beheld him with disbelief and confusion. "What did you say?" she asked, her voice a broken thread. She couldn't have heard him right.

He chuckled. It was a far-from-happy sound—more one of self-scorn. "If you were a control freak, you'd have come after me. I left a wide-enough trail. My lawyer knew where I was staying. All you had to do was ask him." He smoothed her hair, adding, "And why do you think I took the damned red Porsche and parked it practically on Main? It was like a beacon screaming 'I'm here, I'm here.' I wanted to see if you'd come find me and demand my love."

Her obvious shock made him chuckle again—this time with a tinge of real humor. "Pretty egocentric of me, I know." He sobered. "But you didn't come."

Aly frowned, confused. She tried to speak, couldn't. Tried once more. "So—so you salved your bruised ego with—by dating a pretty woman?"

His brows grew together in puzzlement. "Dating . . . ?"

She swallowed the grudging bile that had risen in her throat. "Aunt Merle interrupted your tête-à-tête. Remember?"

"Oh—yes," he acknowledged with a slow nod. Then, to her complete surprise, he grinned. Really grinned. "Maggie Connery."

Aly winced. "Thanks. I really wanted to know her name."

The tone of her voice made him study her more closely. "I hope," he murmured, "that was jealousy I heard."

She struggled, mortified and yanked free from his arms. "Why? Does your ego require it? The old fling has to be jealous of the new one! That's *sick*," she shot back sadly.

He took hold of her shoulders, firmly but gently, and ground out, "Aly, darling, Maggie—" He shook his head and began again, more softly, "Remember once, I told you I fired a woman who was pregnant?"

She nodded dumbly, wondering at his wild subject swing.

"Well," he said with a wry half smile. "That was Maggie. Truth be told, she was a thorn in my side, always disagreeing with my management decisions. But she's a damn fine aeronautical engineer. I wasn't dating her, you little goose," he insisted with a gentle shake. "I was offering her a job with my new firm. I want the best, and Maggie's one of the best. Besides, I owed her one."

Before Aly could absorb his statement, he gathered her close, rasping against her hair, "It's a flight-safety-development firm. The concept's always been a dream of mine—to make flying even more safe than it is. Maggie has an interest in better in-flight detection of wind sheers. Something I want to tackle, too. Together with a couple of other friends in the business, I'll make that dream a reality. The four of us are going to devise mechanisms for safer air traffic, so people like Megan and Pearl won't . . ." His whisper died away, further explanation unnecessary.

"You're starting a business?" she echoed, incredulous.

He held her close, murmuring against her temple. "A job, you might say." Kissing her deeply, he added, "I have a job and socks. Now will you marry me? Or does the fact that you didn't come after me mean you don't love me?"

She held herself slightly away from him to gaze into his expectant face. "You're not going to get after me for needing to be in control?" she asked, hope in her voice. "You realize I have Jenna, Mother, Aunt Merle depending on me. Jack's debts, George—"

"*We* have, sweetheart," he corrected, smiling genuinely. "I've never known a single mother up close. Never understood what women like you have to go through just to survive. You're not perfect, my love," he teased. "But I won't ask you to be, if you don't ask it of me. Do you love me or not?"

"I—I . . ." Her throat was so dry she couldn't talk. All this was too new, too crazy to be true. Did he really have a job? Was he really ready to settle down and be a normal man—a man with ideals?

"Oh," he said, drawing her back. "One other thing. I've decided to donate Mother's mansion for use as an economical place for working mothers to bring their children. A Rountree-subsidized operation on a sliding pay schedule according to the woman's ability to pay." With a finger to her chin, he forced her to meet his eyes. "Because of you, Aly, I've seen how tough it is for working mothers on a budget to cope. What do you think about the Pearl Rountree Memorial Day Care Center?"

She felt a rush of overpowering joy wash through her, and she melted against him, sighing, "I'm dreaming. This can't be real. You can't be real...."

"Marry me, and I'll show you just how real I am," he promised, his voice going rough with desire. "Do you love me, Aly?"

Tears came to her eyes. He was serious—about everything. Job, roots, altruisms. She couldn't find a grain of fault with his desire to honor his little girl. She blinked to clear her vision, and in his gaze she could see that he cherished her fiercely, and that he was dealing with his grief and guilt. She could sense that he was ready to start a new, productive life; one of his own choosing—not his father's.

And, Aly was doubly thrilled to discover that she was to play a major role in that life—that she already had. She smiled timidly up at his expectant face, curled her arms about his wide shoulders and vowed, "I love you, Rourk. I've loved you so long...."

He kissed her. "That's all I needed to hear, sweetheart. I'm a happy man."

"But, Rourk," she interjected worriedly, "I may be out of town a lot of weekends. I like the auction business."

"Jenna and I may be with you—out of town—a lot of weekends," he returned with a sexy rasp.

"You wouldn't mind?"

He kissed the tip of her nose. "If you don't mind socks, why would I mind being with you on weekends?"

"But your job."

"Strictly eight-to-five."

She hugged him close, savoring the moment, wondering if it could possibly really be true. "I won't hold you to that eight-to-five thing. New businesses take work," she relented.

"I've already told my junior Yuppie partners they'd be doing the overtime. What about the socks?"

A giggle of pure happiness bubbled in her throat. "I won't hold you to that, either."

Kissing her firmly, he husked, "This marriage may just work."

She shivered. It was a nice shock to realize that he had imperfections she could accept—even delight in. And once realizing that, she was suddenly much more self-accepting. She had faults. Maybe she was too controlling at times. She'd work on it. Obviously, Rourk was working on his flaws—trying very hard—and she loved him all the more for it.

"*Somethin'* better start working, 'cause Aly sure ain't!" shouted Aunt Merle from very close by. Aly jumped and jerked around in time to see her aunt grab up the cellular phone and roar into it, "Everybody hear that? Unless I can pry these two apart, the auction may have to be postponed till after the wedding. I'll do my best, though," she assured in a snickering bellow, "'cause I've heard how ugly a disappointed condom-tin crowd can get!"

Realizing they'd been overheard in the ballroom, Aly gave Rourk an abashed glance. "I'd better go," she mouthed without sound.

With one last kiss, he nodded and released her.

She took a step away, then turned back. "You realize they're going to tease me unmercifully in there."

He smiled with encouragement. "I'll run interference if you'd like."

She shook her head and smiled back. "No, thanks. But I love you for offering."

"When you need me, I'll be here." He winked, and her world tottered precariously at the love she saw in his face.

"Me, too," she promised, feeling oddly shy, unsure that she deserved such unqualified devotion. Well, she told herself, she'd have to work on that damaged self-image, too. But she knew in her heart that Rourk would be there to help her mend, as she would be for him.

Then with Merle's rather unsubtle throat-clearing, Aly scurried away, her step as buoyant as the clouds that scudded overhead in the sultry early-September sky.

THAT NIGHT, after everyone was gone and Aunt Merle, Maude and Jenna were tucked away in bed, Aly went outside on the patio to drink up the tranquillity of the place.

Rourk had gone back into downtown Wichita to meet with his business partners and tie up some loose ends. She didn't know when he'd be back, but in her heart, she knew he would.

The door to the patio clicked open and her heart thrilled. Without turning, she knew it was him. "Hello, darling," she whispered faintly.

"Hello, Aly," he said, his tone low and loving.

She turned to face him and smiled. "How did your day go?"

They smiled at each other, amused to hear themselves sounding like an old married couple. But Aly really felt that way—suddenly filled with trust and a new sense of security. It was almost like a miracle.

"My day was fine," Rourk replied, walking toward her. "And yours?"

"We made a few million today."

"That's nice," he teased. "What's for dinner?"

"I don't cook very well," she warned, lifting her face for a kiss.

"I can't agree." He nuzzled her throat. "I've been witness to some pretty sexy cookin' on your part, young lady."

She giggled. "That tickles, Rourk." She gently pressed him away. "We can eat later. Right now, I have a collection of my own I thought you'd be interested in."

A raven-hued brow lifted in question. "You think so?"

She grinned impishly. "I know so."

Now, totally secure in the fact that Rourk had never really been a weak man—only a man late in finding himself—she began to unbutton her blouse, taunting, "Sit down on the bench and I'll show it to you."

He did as was asked of him, leaning against the dogwood tree and crossing his arms as he watched her disrobe in engrossed silence.

As the blouse fluttered to the ground, she asked, "Bored yet?"

His lips quirked. "Can't say that I am. No."

She unhooked her skirt and it soon followed the blouse, then her slip was pulled swiftly away over her head, falling unheeded into the pond.

Rourk's eyes widened appreciatively, and Aly couldn't suppress a smile at the success of her feminine wiles. She was wearing a sexy bra, a see-through wisp of black lace nothing, a black-lace garter belt and hose. Rourk swallowed and murmured a frustrated blasphemy. "Hell, woman, what do you collect, men who die of heart attacks?"

She placed her hands on her hips and teased, "Don't be silly. I collect sexy underthings. I went to my apartment and picked up a few to—show you. Thought you might enjoy a glimpse."

With a lusty growl, he vaulted up, hauling her into a powerful embrace, muttering huskily, "What will you take for it?"

Molding herself to him, she whispered, "Everything you have—you sexy devil...."

As he lifted her into his arms and carted her to bed, she laughed gaily, knowing full well that Rourk Rountree was every inch man enough to pay her price, again and again and again—for the rest of their lives....

HARLEQUIN PRESENTS®

is

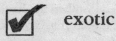

- ✓ exotic
- ✓ dramatic
- ✓ sensual
- ✓ exciting
- ✓ contemporary
- ✓ a fast, involving read
- ✓ terrific!!

Harlequin Presents—
passionate romances
around the world!

PRESENTS-Z

HARLEQUIN ROMANCE®

is

 contemporary
and up-to-date

 heartwarming

 romantic

 exciting

 involving

 fresh and
delightful

 a short, satisfying
read

 wonderful!!

*Today's Harlequin
Romance—the traditional
choice!*